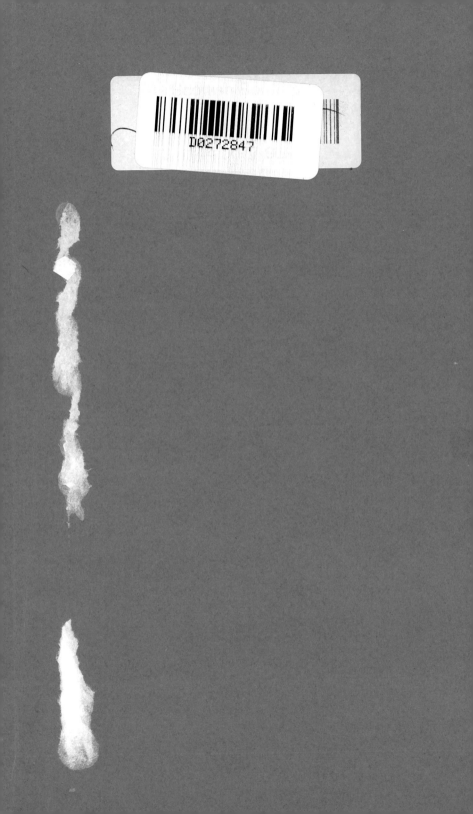

PENGUIN BOOKS

The Bride's Farewell

Praise for *How I Live Now*:

'A crunchily perfect knock-out of a debut novel' – *Guardian*

'This is a powerful novel: timeless and luminous' – *Observer*

'That rare, rare thing, a first novel with a sustained, magical and utterly faultless voice' – Mark Haddon, author of *The Curious Incident of the Dog in the Night-Time*

'Unforgettable . . . Rosoff achieves a remarkable feat' – *Sunday Times*

'Gripping and powerful' – *Independent*

'Intense and startling . . . heartbreakingly romantic' – *The Times*

'A wonderfully original voice' – *Mail on Sunday*

'Readers won't just read this book, they will let it possess them' – *Sunday Telegraph*

'It already feels like a classic, in the sense that you can't imagine a world without it' – *New Statesman*

'Fresh and original' – *Time Out*

Praise for *Just in Case*:

'A modern *Catcher in the Rye* . . . written with generosity and warmth but also with an edgy, unpredictable intelligence' – *The Times*

'Unusual and engrossing' – *Independent*

'Intelligent, ironic and darkly funny' – *Time Out*

'Extraordinary' – *Observer*

'No one writes the way Meg Rosoff does – as if she's thrown away the rules. I love her fizzy honesty, her pluck, her way of untangling emotion through words' – Julie Myerson

Books by Meg Rosoff

HOW I LIVE NOW

JUST IN CASE

WHAT I WAS

THE BRIDE'S FAREWELL

PENGUIN BOOKS

Published by the Penguin Group
Penguin Books Ltd, 80 Strand, London WC2R ORL, England
Penguin Group (USA) Inc., 375 Hudson Street, New York, New York 10014, USA
Penguin Group (Canada), 90 Eglinton Avenue East, Suite 700, Toronto, Ontario, Canada M4P 2Y3
(a division of Pearson Penguin Canada Inc.)
Penguin Ireland, 25 St Stephen's Green, Dublin 2, Ireland (a division of Penguin Books Ltd)
Penguin Group (Australia), 250 Camberwell Road, Camberwell, Victoria 3124, Australia
(a division of Pearson Australia Group Pty Ltd)
Penguin Books India Pvt Ltd, 11 Community Centre, Panchsheel Park, New Delhi – 110 017, India
Penguin Group (NZ), 67 Apollo Drive, Rosedale, North Shore 0632, New Zealand
(a division of Pearson New Zealand Ltd)
Penguin Books (South Africa) (Pty) Ltd, 24 Sturdee Avenue, Rosebank, Johannesburg 2196, South Africa

Penguin Books Ltd, Registered Offices: 80 Strand, London WC2R ORL, England

penguin.com

First published 2009
1

Text copyright © Meg Rosoff, 2009
All rights reserved

Set in 11.9/16pt Sabon by Palimpsest Book Production Limited, Grangemouth, Stirlingshire
Made and printed in England by Clays Ltd, St Ives plc

British Library Cataloguing in Publication Data
A CIP catalogue record for this book is available from the British Library

HARDBACK
ISBN: 978-0-141-38393-4

TRADE PAPERBACK
ISBN: 978-0-141-38394-1

www.greenpenguin.co.uk

Penguin Books is committed to a sustainable future
for our business, our readers and our planet.
The book in your hands is made from paper
certified by the Forest Stewardship Council.

MEG ROSOFF

The *Bride's Farewell*

PENGUIN BOOKS

For Ann and Liz

1

On the morning she was to be married, Pell Ridley crept up from her bed in the dark, kissed her sisters goodbye, fetched Jack in from the wind and rain on the heath and told him they were leaving. Not that he was likely to offer any objections, being a horse.

There wasn't much to take. Bread and cheese and a bottle of ale, a clean apron, a rope for Jack and a book belonging to Mam with pictures of birds drawn in soft pencil, which no one ever looked at but her. The dress in which she was to be married she left untouched, spread over a dusty chair.

She felt carefully inside the best teapot for the coins put away for her dowry, slipped the rope round Jack's neck and turned to go.

Head down, squinting into the rain, she stopped short at the sight of a ghostly figure in the path. It had as little substance as a moth, but its eyes burned a hole in the dark.

'Go back to bed, Bean.'

It didn't budge.

She sighed, noticing how the pale oval of a face remained stubbornly set.

'Please, Bean. Go home.' *Oh God*, she thought, *no*. But it was no use appealing to God about something already decided.

Without waiting to be invited, the boy scrambled up on to Jack, and with no other option she pulled herself up behind him, feeling the warmth of his thin body against her own. And so it was, with a resigned chirrup to Jack and no tear in her eye, that they set off down the hill, heading north, which at that moment appeared to be the exact direction in which lay the rest of the world.

'I'm sorry, Birdie,' whispered the girl, with a final thought for the husband that should have been. Perhaps at the last minute he would find another bride. Perhaps he would marry Lou. Anyone will do, she thought. As long as it isn't me.

2

The open road. What a trio of words. What a vision of blue sky and untouched hills and narrow trails heading God knew where and being free – free and hungry, free and cold, free and wet, free and lost – who could mourn such conditions, faced with the alternative?

They'd been on the road barely an hour when the night began to thin and they came to a village identical to the one they'd just left – one road in, one road out and one longer, less-trodden path that circled round. Every soul in that place knew Pell well enough to know she shouldn't be up and riding away from home at dawn on her wedding day, so she steered Jack wide and skirted each village till the names grew strange and the people they passed started to look unfamiliar. Even then, to be certain, they kept on, stopping only once under a tree for a meal of brown bread and beer.

Bean rode even when Pell slid off to walk, his frame so slight she doubted the horse noticed him at all. When she felt overcome by gloom and doubt and astonishment at what she'd done, he smiled encouragement at her, but most of the time he sat silent, looking straight ahead.

'Don't you want to go home, Bean?' Her idea of freedom had not included him.

But he shook his head, and Pell sighed. What's done is done, she thought, and no use looking back.

They were headed for the horse fair at Salisbury. It was less a plan than a starting point, but it led them into the great anonymous bulk of England where an infinite number of possible lives beckoned. Away from Nomansland, away from Mam and Pa. Away from Birdie Finch.

'He'll make a good steady husband,' her sister Lou had told her, more than once. 'And you like him well enough already.'

'But I can ride and shoe a horse better than he can.'

'Is that your best objection?' Lou wished someone would look at her the way Birdie looked at Pell.

'It will have to do,' Pell laughed, and wheeled her horse off across the heath.

Lou watched them go, pressing her lips together with disapproval.

Everyone knew Birdie and Pell would be married. They'd been betrothed practically from birth, or at least from the first time she'd ridden a horse, just after she learned to walk, set up behind Birdie and holding on for dear life. That pony had no time for children, but Birdie stuck to him and Pell stuck to Birdie, first like brother and sister, and later with her head buried in his shoulder and her arms round his waist.

'When we're grown,' he'd say, 'you'll be married to the finest blacksmith in two counties.'

'You ought to marry Lou,' Pell answered. 'She's the one wants a husband.'

He looked at her, injured. 'I've nothing to say to your sister, and you know it.'

She couldn't contradict him, for it was true that Lou hated

4

mud and horses equally, was the least likely person to attend a difficult calving or grab hold of a pony's mane and swing up on to its back.

There was a time – an early time – when the thought of marrying Birdie had made Pell proud, not least for besting Lou, whom everyone knew would make the better wife. In those days, boy and girl spent every spare moment together, from first dawn till last light, and there wasn't a horse they couldn't catch, ride and tame. Before she was old enough to know what kissing was, he'd kissed her and said, 'There now, that means we'll be married someday.' And at first she believed him because she wanted to and later because she couldn't think of anything else to believe.

'On *that* spot,' he said one day, pointing to the empty field just beyond his parents' house. 'That's where we'll build our house, and fill it to bursting with children.' He held his arms out wide, to indicate multitudes.

Pell stared at him. A house full of children? She had only to look at her mother – worn and shapeless with a leaking bladder, great knotted blue veins, and breasts flat as old wineskins – to reject that plan. And worse, even, than the physical toll was the grinding disappointment, the drudgery, the changelessness of life in this place.

Toil and hardship and a clamour of mouths to feed? Not now, Pell thought. Not ever.

3

In late afternoon, they came to a hamlet comprised of four thatched wooden houses and two more made of cob. Pell stopped outside the one with the nicest garden, where a girl her own age fed soured milk and slops to the family pig. The girl had a face already pulled inwards with troubles, but she wiped her hands on her apron and set down the bucket when she saw Pell. They considered each other while passing the time, one wondering who was the stranger with a child and a white horse, and what was she doing here, the other happy to observe a life of feeding slops to a pig, as long as it wasn't her life.

'Are you travelling alone?' asked the girl, though she might have answered that question on the evidence of her own eyes. When Pell indicated Bean, she looked surprised. 'What, no father or husband?'

Pell shook her head. 'I have no husband and never will.' She was pleased to speak the words out loud.

The girl's sour mouth dropped open, and without warning turned up in a smile. She offered Bean and Jack apples from her apron, as she'd plenty. 'He's handsome,' she said, admiring Jack and murmuring, 'you're handsome you are.' Then to Bean: 'What's your name?'

Bean stared at her, silent and unflinching.

'Is he right in the head?'

Pell felt insulted for him, but said yes, and then volunteered that they were on their way to Salisbury fair to look for work, and watched the other girl's expression. Proper girls didn't declare their intention never to marry, followed by a plan to go to Salisbury with nothing but an odd boy and a horse for company.

Why, she'd never heard the like.

A silence fell between them and Pell was about to move on when the girl held out her hand to Jack once more with an apple, as if to delay their departure by a moment or two. Jack lowered his head and took it softly, and Pell smiled and let him finish before setting off. Even then he dragged his feet, and the girl stared after Pell in a way that said she didn't think it right what Pell was doing, being out in the world on her own like that, but on the other hand she wished it was her.

All along the road they passed empty farms, abandoned to the promise of more money and better lives in city factories and railway yards. At one of these places, in an empty barn, the travellers set down for the night in perfect isolation.

Bean slid off Jack while Pell opened her bag for the old woven blanket she meant to have as a bed, and discovered folded within it a beautiful fine-knitted shawl, large and warm and charcoal brown, made from the wool of new black lambs. The shawl was as good as a message from her sister saying she should use it instead of a husband to keep warm in the world.

Pell wondered how Lou had known her secret. Such was the way with sisters, the knowledge of the other that bound them up in love and hate. Lou could marry Birdie now that her sister had run away, which would have been for Mam a source of deep and lasting satisfaction. It would prove to her that the fates shared her taste for Louisa over Pell, though in fact the fates did not.

Birdie wouldn't mind which of the sisters he married, despite them being as unlike as fire and clay. His need of a wife was the same as his need of a new suit of clothing or an acre of maize. So Pell told herself.

'Come along, Bean,' she said. And then she wrapped him in the beautiful woollen shawl and settled him into a deep bed of straw, where he nestled down like a calf, falling instantly asleep. Pell watched him and thought of Lou knitting, her quick fingers carding and spinning and looping the soft brown wool. It had been made for her wedding, that much Pell guessed, and she was grateful for it now. The boy shivered a little in his sleep and there was nothing for it but to cover him with more straw and add the other blanket for warmth. He would present no problem, she knew, would demand nothing and express no dissatisfaction with whatever came his way. He had come away for the same reason she had, there being nothing left for him at home.

She tethered Jack, and wriggled down into the straw beside Bean so that the shawl enveloped them both. The little boy and the soft wool smelled of home, of everything she loved and longed to escape.

They were lucky. It was a good place to sleep, dry and snug, and though she cried for a time and held Bean close, before long it was morning and the first night had passed not much less comfortably than usual and somewhat more so without six other souls attending her every move.

4

The light still came early at this time of year, and they awoke in the soft gold of dawn. Jack dozed while Pell rubbed her face with a handkerchief and water, combed her dark hair and plaited it in one thick braid down the centre of her back. It might have been a wasted effort, trying to look respectable with her bare feet and legs brown from the sun. But if people took her for a gypsy, well then, she would tell futures to get by.

Having finished her rough version of a toilette she attempted to smooth Bean's hair and find his features under a layer of dust but he shook his head and fled out of reach and in the end she gave up trying.

They began to walk again, cheered by the road curling up towards Salisbury. It was little travelled, too narrow for a horse and cart and loud with birdsong. Through the shade of ancient oaks and dappled beech groves they walked, Pell leading, ducking her head to avoid the long arms of flowering bramble. She walked barefoot to save boot leather, and sudden patches of sunlight trembled beneath her feet, warming the crumbly soil. At unfamiliar sounds she started, and looked back down the path, though she doubted anyone would think to follow them here.

Mostly they travelled in silence, the regular *thud-ump* of her horse's tread familiar as the beat of her own heart. They passed a farmer she recognized slightly but it had been years since they'd last met and the woman shape of her was a perfect disguise. He said, 'Hello, nice day,' and she did too, and maybe he peered at her and the boy and wondered for an instant, but that was all. The freedom of being nobody after all those years of everyone knowing exactly who she was made the blood in her veins run a little wild.

They stopped in one village where Pell paid a few pence to buy bread from a woman selling heavy brown loaves still warm from the oven and cheese she made herself. The woman looked at her without sympathy.

'What are you doing on the road all alone?'

Pell wondered for a moment whether Bean was visible only to her. 'I'm going to Salisbury,' she answered.

'For what?' snapped the woman.

Pell's pale face and dark eyes belied the heat of her blood. 'There's no work at home,' she said evenly, and stopped herself adding, *and that's just the start of the troubles there.*

'Hmmph,' said the woman, staring at Pell hard, reading the quality of her horse and her clean face, the worn-out wool of her pinafore and the odd brother, and knowing the girl's history from what she read. She had seen almost every human story pass by over the years.

When Pell unwrapped her parcel sometime later there was an extra slab pressed in against the one she'd bought, an additional thick slice cut off the new round cheese. Both pieces were sweating, pale yellow, and tasted of milk, and Pell felt a rush of gratitude for the unexpected kindness.

In early afternoon, another woman came running after her

panting, and asked if she'd be so good as to post a letter, given that she was going past the village post office in any case, and when Pell nodded the woman produced an envelope and smoothed it flat as if wishing it luck on its way. She pressed a penny for the stamp into Pell's hand, with the explanation that the letter was 'for my son in London'.

Pell nodded again and didn't say a word, but the woman couldn't help puffing herself up a little and adding proudly, 'He's gone there to seek his fortune.'

At that, Pell's heart dipped in sympathy. She had a fair idea of how the story of the son's fortune might go, thinking of next door's son coming back after a year in the big city factories hungrier and thinner than when he left, with tales of cruelty and hardship to freeze your soul.

Pell would have liked to speak more to the woman, to prolong her moment of hopefulness, but Bean sat forward and chirped to Jack, loosening his rein and moving off, so she had to follow. She looked back to wave, and saw the woman still standing, watching, reluctant to let the letter out of her sight.

Pell turned to the road ahead once more and closed her eyes. A vision of Salisbury fair filled her head, with nothing beyond.

5

By mid-afternoon, they had joined the highway, where a slow trickle of humanity headed for the fair. From every direction they came, in caravans, traps and farmer's carts, on foot in little chattering groups, or all alone dragging heavy loads. As the day wore on, the trickle became a stream and the stream a river. Some rode or led or drove horses in strings or pairs, and Pell was glad Jack wasn't the kicking sort, but only huffed once or twice at mares he fancied as they passed.

It became difficult to manoeuvre, and when a thickset young farmer backed his horse into Jack, Pell turned to him smiling, in expectation of an apology. Instead, he leaned in close to her and whispered, 'What're *you* selling?' with a smile that made the blood rise in her face.

She reined Jack hard, cutting through the crowd and setting off a volley of complaints. Behind her the farmer laughed unpleasantly, and Pell forced her mind away from him to the happy distraction of horses bound for market. Some were driven, some ridden and some led; some strode past graceful as gods, others looked broken down and ready for the knacker's yard. There were greys and bays, chestnuts and roans, Roman noses and deep chests and high bony withers, but most were just big honest beasts looking for a good home with someone who would work decent hours beside them and feed them decent food. Which was what the men wanted too.

At least half of the horses on the road were coloured gypsy types splashed all over black or brown and white with big domed heads and feathery legs. But even among so many the same, there were gaits and heads that drew your eye and said *look at me*.

And Jack as good as any she saw and better, Pell thought.

Passing through a little village and over a narrow wooden bridge, Pell found herself riding beside a middle-aged man with a pleasant face, who, after some time and one or two sidelong glances, ventured a conversation.

'That's a very fine pony you have there, miss.'

Pell continued to look straight ahead as if he hadn't spoken, but his voice sounded friendly and it felt wrong, somehow, to snub him. She offered the smallest of nods.

'Are you taking him to market?'

Below Pell's elbow, Bean craned to look at the man, and smiled encouragement.

The man smiled back. 'It'd be a shame to sell him, now wouldn't it?' He addressed his comments to Bean. 'Or perhaps you're buying?'

With her back straight and chin high, Pell pressed Jack to step out ahead. Bean looked across and shook his head.

The man kept pace. 'May I enquire, then, as to your mission in Salisbury?'

'No,' said Pell primly, and both the man and Bean laughed. Defeated, Pell glanced over at him. From his immaculate green livery she guessed he worked for one of the big houses. His face was round and open and he rode an elegant chestnut mare, leading a matched pair of bays with long necks and fine heads. The three animals claimed more than a full share of his attention, and it showed some horsemanship that he managed to keep in step with Jack.

Pell had prepared a polite rebuff to any further attempts at engagement, but it proved unnecessary, for at that moment a young lady just ahead waved a large white handkerchief to catch the eye of her friend, causing the chestnut to spin sideways, eyes bulging. Another rider would have lost his seat, Pell thought, noticing how quietly her companion followed the mare's temper, how he sat still and calm without leaning on his mount's mouth to right himself. She was a spooky creature, scared of her own shadow and not interested in proving otherwise to anyone. Bean giggled.

'You're sensible wanting rid of her,' Pell said, thinking, That mare's had more than a few guineas wasted on her and will have again.

He glanced over, pleased at eliciting a response at last. 'Aye, but just look at her. There'll always be someone wanting such a fine-looking mare, and willing to take the rest with it.'

'She's fickle as fortune,' murmured Pell.

At that he nodded, adding in a low voice, as if talking to the horse, 'You're right there. But it's hard to blame her, poor thing, for she had a bad fall over a fence with a fool of a rider. How do you tell a horse to settle and trust you after that?'

'You just tell her.'

The thought seemed to amuse him. 'Go on, then.'

Pell rode up, drawing even with the mare's head, then leaned over and spoke softly in her ear. 'That's enough, now –'

'Desdemona.'

Pell looked startled.

'The much-wronged wife from a play by Mr William Shakespeare,' the man said, with a raised eyebrow. 'So I am told.'

Pell laughed. 'All right, then. That's enough, now, Desdemona, you won't fall again.' The mare flicked one ear back to catch the girl's voice. Pell turned to the man once more. 'You see? It's what she's been waiting to hear.'

He laughed softly. 'But who knows if what you've told her is true? Depends to whom she's sold and how she's ridden.'

'Well, then,' Pell said coolly, gazing straight into his eyes, 'she's perfectly right to be anxious, is she not?'

He laughed again, pleased to be bested, and she noticed that his face wasn't a bad face, if you were the sort of girl who cared about such things.

Having established a connection, they rode together companionably, speaking of horses because it was a subject neither seemed likely to exhaust. When the man turned off to claim lodgings at the Queen's Head, Bean looked up into Pell's face as if searching for something. Not finding it, he lowered his gaze and sighed, dejected for reasons he kept to himself.

6

Four worn clay walls and half as many dark low rooms made up the place that Pell called home. Her father built the house himself before he and Mam married, hacking bricks straight out of the ground and piling them up to make walls thick enough to keep out the wind and rain (and the light and warmth of the sun). A roof of heather, reed and mud topped it off, so that in the end it huddled like a heap, nearly invisible at the edge of the hamlet of Nomansland, itself crouched on the very edge of the New Forest as if liable at any moment to tumble down the hill into Wiltshire.

Those lime-washed walls of rubble and straw had moments of charm in summer when honeysuckle and wild roses scrambled up the front and poppies, foxglove and honesty grew every which way from window frames and patches of earth, but inside was damp and crumbling and held the smell of smoke forever so that winters passed in a long succession of near-fatal bronchial ailments. There was one oak chair passed to Mam from her parents, and a wedding clock given by an aunt, now dead, which no longer lent support to the desired illusion of gentility.

'The only hours requiring our attention,' roared a drunken Joe Ridley one night early in their marriage, as he swept the clock from its place of pride above the hearth, 'are those given to man that he may heed the Lord's bidding!'

The clock landed with a sickening crack, and Mam hurried to sweep the poor broken thing up and hide it away.

One room downstairs with a fire and a pantry, and one room upstairs were all Pa had managed to build, twenty years ago when money and drink were in short supply and he still hoped to convert the world to his faith, and Pell's Mam to the view that she hadn't made the direst mistake of her life in marrying him. The hints had all been there if only she'd paid attention: the low ceilings, the walls not straight enough to support proper windows, the chimney built of straw and mud so it caught fire on windy nights. And no shortage of windy nights.

Upstairs there was no fire, but the chimneybreast passed through Mam's side of the room, and on freezing winter nights with the wind and filthy rain seeping in through the thatch and Pa fallen down drunk at the inn, the little girls would sneak one at a time into the marital bed. If Pa snored at home, they'd wrap themselves in blankets on the floor and huddle up together against the warmth of the chimney till morning.

Beside the fire stood a table of hewn oak carved all round with roses, Ridley's wedding present to the young wife whose parents already hated him for his views without any need of discovering precisely what they were. They recognized the few types of marriageable men at a glance, and knew that a passion for God and a meagre glimmer of charm were all that disguised the catastrophic weakness within.

The wedding table was big enough for eight, and rocked – because the floor was not flat or the legs not square, either of which condemned him.

Within a decade, his wife had presented him with enough children to fill the table, stifling the cries of the first time and thereafter squeezing them out with silent resignation. The preacher was proud of his wife and her resistance to death by childbirth, despite the many practical problems her productivity raised. Her forbearance was something to lay claim to, like a hen that laid three seasons out of four, and he took his God-given marital rights without guilt, and occasionally with force. George, James, John and Edward followed Pell and Lou, and after them came Sally, Fran and Ellen. Nine children plus Bean. Four now buried in the churchyard at Lover.

The children went to work as soon as they could walk, according to capacity and inclination: Lou, Sally and Ellen at home with Mam, and Pell up on the heath with Birdie, later followed about by Frannie on a pony no bigger than a dog. In appearance the two sets of girls couldn't have been more different: three always tidy, with hair tied up each night in rag curls, the other two dressed like banshees in torn skirts, with brown legs and hair thick and tangled as a hawthorn hedge.

Edward might have been a scholar had he possessed the foresight to be born into a different family, and was often to be found half hidden in a stand of grass, reading or practising his letters. The girls laughed at him without malice.

'Come for a ride,' Pell would call from the back of her horse, looking for all the world like a centaurine with her bare legs and tangled mane.

Edward gazed up at her admiringly, squinting slightly, and begging her silence with a warning finger pressed against his lips. But he needn't have bothered. She would not give him away to Mam or Pa or Lou or anyone else who might want him for work.

The older Ridley boys showed signs of having inherited their father's appetites, and Nomansland parents guarded their daughters fiercely. Despite proscriptions, however, more than one local girl had been known to pass a pleasant afternoon in the corner of a meadow or barn with George or James or John's mouth pressed to her warm skin.

'Kiss me, you heartless girl,' George begged Birdie's sister, laughing, and then, not waiting for an answer, slid her pinafore up over her waist as she sighed some small protest and breathed his name in little gasps. They were only young, but her father beat the girl soundly on discovery of the game. His subsequent encounter with the Ridley boy was conducted in private, but despite living within spitting distance of each other the boy and girl never spoke again.

Immediately they were old enough, the boys moved into the barn, where there was more space and no chance of catching a glimpse of female flesh. On this point the clergyman was uncharacteristically clear. He would have no obscenity in his house. He would have poverty, violence, drunkenness, starvation and disease, but at any state of undress he most decidedly drew the line. Not that such sights would be likely at the best of times, the change from day to nightclothes being the stuff of wealthier households.

It was a tangle of a family, for better or worse, a right complexity of children, all knotted up with love and jealousy, and all competing for anything they could get – food, boots, underclothes without holes, a shawl, a piece of bread, a kind word from Mam. Each acquisition took on the status of treasure in times so tight you thought you might die for the want of half a spoonful of dripping or a shoe you couldn't see through. But they were accustomed to such conditions and thought nothing particular of them.

7

Pell and Bean approached Salisbury along a busy thoroughfare that traversed half a mile of slums. Beyond the city walls to the north, Pell could see the tip of the lacy cathedral spire rising up towards heaven, while here on earth, stinking sewage collected in ditches beside the road. Drivers slaughtered lame or exhausted animals casually where they fell, then butchered, hung and sold them on the spot to avoid transport into town. Where fowl were killed, feathers thickened the river of blood, and at the corner of every eye lurked the shadowy darting figures of rats. Dirty women and children stood by the road watching the parade, some offering drooping bunches of mint or parsley, ginger beer or pies with grubby pastry for sale. A sheepdog lapped at the foul soup.

When a long dray pulled by eight horses parted the crowd, its load of barrels jostling threateningly on the deep ruts, Jack stumbled and slipped sideways into the ditch. Pell steadied him, but as he clambered out, legs dyed pink to the knee with blood, he splashed stinking water on to the immaculate breeches of a gentleman riding past.

'Keep hold of your horse, for pity's sake,' cried the man, making no attempt to conceal his disgust. He sneered at Pell, pulling a fine linen handkerchief from his pocket, with which to blot the filth.

'Let it be,' said his companion. 'No point ruining your gloves as well.'

For the briefest of moments, Pell saw herself through their eyes – her clothes worn and patched, Jack thickset and countrified in comparison to their mounts, Bean with his odd watchful look. She felt ashamed, despite a conviction that the men were neither braver nor cleverer than she, only luckier in their conditions of birth.

Every inn they passed had horses tied two or three to a box and their owners likewise stacked in haylofts, in rooms above the kitchen, by the root cellar or wherever else they could be packed four to a bed and charged for the privilege. Not that Pell had any intention of staying in a hotel, what with her entire fortune adding up to next to nothing.

She and Bean stopped just outside of the city gates, in an area crowded with ponies and wagons. They found a few square feet of empty space and had just settled in, making themselves as comfortable as possible, when it began to rain. Pell sighed, rolled up their blankets and led Bean and Jack over to a stand of trees where they might be sheltered from the main force of the downpour. Ragged and wet, they stood gazing out on to a large rectangle of trodden dirt and grass, wishing they were elsewhere. All around, gypsy families in bender tents and covered wagons lit fires and called to one another in rapid, incomprehensible patois. Their grim, confident faces frightened Pell.

Another half hour passed, and a skinny girl emerged dripping from the wall of water and tugged at Pell's sleeve. 'Ma says you're to come to us.'

Following the direction of the grubby finger, Pell saw a gypsy woman, lean as a whippet with high cheekbones and thick red hair, her wagon tied up with patched canvas and looking barely more inviting than spending the night soaking wet out of doors. The woman stared at Bean, and Pell hesitated for a moment, wondering what the offer entailed and whether they might be better off in the rain. Warnings against the filthy minds and homes of gypsies had been fed to Ridley's children with their mother's milk; Pell's father considered association with the heathen race an abomination.

But as the torrent showed no sign of abating and her dress and hair streamed water, practicality won out. She nodded thanks and led Jack over to the wagon, where the woman immediately took hold of his headstall, tethering him beside her own horse under a makeshift canvas cover. Pressed up against the big carthorse out of the worst of the downpour, Jack chuntered contentedly while Pell wrung out what clothing she could, hanging the blankets beside a small iron stove that threw out no more than a suggestion of heat. They would dry, given time.

The rain stopped and, as if on signal, the edge of the wagon spilled gypsy children. One of the big girls lit the fire under a three-legged pot, waited for its contents to boil, and then ladled out into bowls. Pell peered at the soup as she passed it along but could detect nothing in it besides turnip, nettle and onion. She cast about for Bean, who squatted beneath the caravan with the skinny girl, prodding a large toad with a stick. Both children were silent, with pale skin and big dark eyes. For the fraction of an instant with the light just so, it was like looking at a single image reflected in a glass.

Recalling her sense of decency, Pell turned and introduced herself and Bean to the gypsy woman, who nodded.

'Esther,' she said. Then pointed to the children. 'Elspeth,

Eammon, Errol, Evelina and Esme.' She smiled grimly. 'Same father for them all.'

Pell scanned the collection of identical features and the children stared back at her without emotion. She judged the eldest to be about twelve, with the hips and breasts of a woman. Esme, the youngest, was slightly taller than Bean. Like him, she had a face made old by hunger.

'He is your son?' Esther indicated Bean.

'My brother.'

Esme emerged from beneath the wagon followed by Bean, whom Esther grabbed and held at arm's length. She studied his face with a curious intensity until he wriggled away out of reach. He turned back to stare.

Esther looked from Pell to Bean and back again, her gaze shrewd. 'You have the same mother and father?'

The question startled Pell. 'No. Pa took him in as a baby. From a parishioner too poor to raise him.'

Esther nodded. A dense silence flowed between her and the little boy.

'Does he ever speak?'

Pell shook her head.

'Mute in the family's considered lucky. Absorbs all the bad fortune, so they say.'

'Not so lucky for him, then.'

'No.' Esther's laugh was harsh. And then, 'Have you something for the little ones?'

Pell reached into her bag and pulled out the remainder of her bread, which the woman secreted in the large pocket of her apron. Once the meal was finished it was easier to look and judge the state of the wagon, which was warm enough, with the musky smell of too many children. And when Pell did (far too late) check in every dark corner for predatory men, there were none, only a few untidy piles of belongings.

Plates were rinsed in a bucket of rainwater outside the wagon, and the children drifted inside one by one. Elspeth, the eldest, presided while the rest settled side by side on feed bags stuffed with straw, some head to tail and some not. To her surprise, Pell saw Bean crammed in among them, though it took a moment to determine which child he was. His head rested on Esme's skinny arm, and he looked more peaceful than he had since they'd left Nomansland. Pell realized all at once how little she replaced the crowded family at home, and wondered what his decision to accompany her had cost him.

She made a space in between the pots and pans at the side of the wagon, wrapped herself in her shawl, tucked her purse into the front of her dress and settled down to sleep. The drip drip drip of rain running on canvas didn't disturb her, for she was dry enough and could lift the cover an inch or two and whisper to Jack, who puffed a little through his nostrils in return.

Sleep came right away. When she awoke in the night, Esther was snoring opposite, tucked up with one of the children muttering softly by her side. Pell thought how strange it was to swap one family for another, and how effortlessly the conversion seemed to have occurred.

Just before sunrise came the smell of smoke fires, a clamour of voices and the general clanking and clattering of pots and wagons, and of men ready to pull up stakes and move on. Shaking the sleep from her head, Pell checked first on Bean and Esme – their position unchanged from the night before – then pushed out into the damp air to greet Jack. He looked in fine spirits after his night under cover, luxury for a horse who'd spent his whole life out of doors leaning into a gale.

Torn between gratitude and self-interest, Pell produced a wedge of cheese, hidden away for later, and shared it out among the children for breakfast. They swallowed it down quick as stoats and stared hard at her with rapacious eyes.

As the sun rose over the horizon, the gypsy family put out their fire and packed up the caravan in minutes, ready to set off before Pell had even finished her tea. She wondered at their talent for quick departures and what circumstances had honed the skill. Bean looked from Pell to Esme, reluctant to say goodbye to his new friend, and when Esther suggested they meet later that day by the cathedral, Pell agreed. Bean ran alongside and waved until the caravan entered the great stone arch in the city wall, and was swallowed up in the crowd.

8

As soon as they emerged from babyhood, the male Ridleys hired out as farm labourers, taking turns to trail behind their father from village to village, reluctant acolytes in the art of religious hectoring. Edward hid whenever his father was at home, would rather take a beating than accompany him out preaching.

At home, with their mother in a near-constant state of lying-in, Lou and Ellen had responsibility for the carding, knitting and plaiting (for hats and baskets), the cooking and mending, the churning, cheese making and bread baking. Bean's delicate fingers made fine straight plaits that fetched a good price at market, while Sally, lame from birth, sat and knitted, her stubby fingers counting the stitches of fine stockings and jerseys and drawers.

Pell and Frannie gathered wood for the fire, fetched water from the well and tended the cow and pig, when they weren't out on the heath shearing and milking and herding for Birdie's father. With what Pell and the boys earned out of doors, and all that Lou, Bean, Ellen and Sally accomplished at home, the pantry would be filled for winter with fruit in jars, apples set on racks, potatoes in the clamp, hanging bacon, and maize flour ground arduously by hand to save paying the miller. But no matter how they picked and pickled, preserved and bottled and saved, there never was enough to feed them all through the long cold winters, so that each new child was born into hunger, a hunger that barely deserved a second thought.

'Look what I have for you,' Frannie cried one fine spring day, tumbling in through the doorway clutching a basket bigger than herself filled with wool.

Sally scrutinized the raw fleeces, prodding them with a disdainful finger. 'I'll have them when they're clean,' she said with a frown, turning her back on the younger girl.

'I'm to catch and shear and wash them too?' Frannie snorted. 'I'll have your job instead.'

'All right then, it's yours,' declared Sally, hurling a half-knitted stocking at her.

Frannie picked up the work and examined it: perfect, without a single false stitch. To her credit, she surrendered at once. 'My stockings would make us all lame,' she declared, giggling, and raced out of the door without a backward glance.

And so, Sally was left with the grease wool. She hauled the heavy basket up with a sigh and limped out of the house to the lean-to barn where she found Lou and Ellen churning milk. Lou peered over into the basket. 'What are we expected to do with *that*?' She poked a finger at the filthy wool.

'Frannie ought to clean it.'

'Yes, and I suppose she will – once the lambs and foals are born and fed and weaned, and old enough to fend for themselves, and if we're all still alive and haven't forgotten the job altogether. Then, perhaps.'

'She says she fancies my job because it's easier,' said Sally, her face sulky, and Lou kissed her.

'Never mind, sweet. She fancies herself a boy as well, and that's no nearer true.'

Ellen looked on with interest. Older only than Bean, she made a feature of not attracting attention. In the scrabbling scrum of siblings, Ellen was the most reluctant to claim ground for herself, to instigate a row or take sides in a complaint. Soft where Frannie was angular, slow where Sally was brisk, Lou loved her for her dreamy eyes, and kept her close.

In the absence of a serviceable parent, Lou fussed over the little ones, soothed their feelings and taught them all the manners and skills she knew. Thanks mainly to her efforts, there were times – with ponies in the garden, plums on the table, sun on the front wall, and Pa with the boys a day's or a week's walk away – that happiness nudged at the cottage walls. All the joy that any of them could remember was lit by the low slow dwindling light of long June evenings with work finished and nothing urgent to do but knit and talk or race back and forth across the heath on horseback.

On winter nights when he wasn't drunk, and sometimes when he was, Pa schooled George, James, Edward and John in reading and Bible and history and how to add up numbers and preach to an empty church. Of the boys, only Edward paid attention to book learning. But Pell sat with her back to him, plaiting straw for hats and going over each lesson in her head, while George and John made faces and pinched each other and James prayed to God to be somewhere else.

Mam didn't hold by schooling. 'Turns out boys too clever to be useful,' she said, 'and girls no good to marry.' Well, and wasn't she just the perfect example? Ignorant as a thistle, married to a drunk and pushing out baby after baby, each of which had to be clothed and fed until it grew up and left, or died.

No one in the parish was what you might call well off, and by the time Pell turned ten, she and Lou had an expertise in stretching ends past straining point in an ever-hopeful and ever-futile attempt to make them meet. It was a skill practised by every child in Nomansland and each learned it from its Mam who had, of course, learned the same way.

The only thing of which there was no shortage was ponies. As commoners, Birdie's family had ownership and responsibility in equal measure – for herding and marking and selling the horses in good times, and for finding enough food to keep them alive in bad. But each horse needed trimmed feet and the ones that worked required shoes, and that made more than enough work for William Finch, and every other farrier in the parish.

It was for this reason that Birdie's father took on whichever Ridley girls were available to work, and gladly, for they were cheaper to employ than boys, and hard workers. As the years passed, however, the decision caused him some unease. For despite the bloodlines of his own children, each a pure horseman dating back ten generations, William Finch could not help but notice that the quickest learners, the best workers, and the children with the greatest natural affinity for the job did not belong to him.

9

Once inside Salisbury's walls, Pell and Bean competed with half the population to cross roads crammed with the other half. Everywhere, fierce desperate little dogs raced back and forth, nipping and growling at the hocks of sheep and cattle to stop them stampeding down the long sloping chute of a high street. Jack pricked his ears forward, tossed his head and danced crab-ways. There were so many sights to take in, so many people, so many varieties of bread and cheese and pie and ale and sweets; so many villains, cheats and players, vagrants, opportunists, showmen and bawds. Salisbury was unnerving for a country horse, and exhilarating too. Jack longed to plunge headlong into the chaos and add to it.

It seemed as if the entire equine world had found its way to the horse fair. Men led big carthorses harnessed by twos and fours with polished brass and gleaming leather, brood mares still suckling late foals, and stallions available for stud. And always some boy galloped full tilt with nothing but a bit of rope for a bridle, scattering all manner of panicked creatures in his wake. Pell saw a child escape death by half an inch under the wheels of a wagon, while a big handsome white bull with a ring through his nose – docile as a lamb one moment – turned and ripped open the belly of a screaming carthorse the next. Some of the younger boys cheered for the bull as the poor horse's entrails sagged from the wound and the awful smell of organs came to Pell in a gust so strong she could taste it. The brawl that followed was fuelled by blood and mud and looked certain to end in more death.

She turned Jack away from the scene just as her father entered Salisbury through St Ann's gate in search of his renegade children. They passed within twenty yards of each other on either side of the frumenty-seller's striped tent – Pell and Bean heading towards the grounds of the cathedral, Joe Ridley to the nearest tavern.

In the cathedral close, among the restless horses and old-looking children, Pell found Esther camped near to a man and wife, not young, with a splay-footed cob tethered to an ancient wagon. For an instant Pell wondered why Esther had chosen to stop here, away from the gypsy encampment. But an instant later the thought was gone, dissolved in the hectic air.

Leading Jack, Pell asked politely if the old couple minded her taking the spot next to theirs, and seeing how young she was, with a boy they took to be her own and no husband in evidence, they took pity on her and granted their assent. They were glad to have a girl set down between the gypsy wagon and their own, despite the questions raised by the fatherless child. The couple were Mr and Mrs Bewes, and pleased to make her acquaintance.

'This is Bean,' Pell told them, letting go of him at last as he struggled away after his new friend.

'An unusual moniker,' said the woman, drawing her eyebrows together. 'Named after his pa, was he?' She was fishing, unable to settle for so little information.

'No,' Pell said, but on second thought smiled, not wishing to sow suspicion where she needed friends. 'He is my brother. The youngest of five.'

'Five brothers!' crowed Mrs Bewes, hands clutched to her breast. 'What a comfort for your poor dear mother.'

Pell did not explain their circumstances further.

'And you are here to buy a horse? Or to sell one?' Mrs Bewes looked at Jack.

I am in need of work, Pell thought. I left home in a hurry. My brothers are dead and my mother has only Lou and the little girls at home.

I will never, ever marry.

A knot of panic formed near her heart. What could she say to this woman? She forced herself to smile. 'We are seeking . . .' She glanced at Bean, out of earshot. 'To buy. Perhaps.'

'Well, then, without a doubt you've come to the right place.' Mr Bewes looked kindly at her, but his wife merely nodded. If the condition of the girl's clothing was anything to go by, money was not plentiful at home. Perhaps she was hoping for a bargain, or a miracle.

'*We* have come in search of a nice solid pony, strong enough to pull a plough but not so heavy he can't be rode to the next village in the dead of night,' said Mrs Bewes. She informed Pell that she was a midwife, still active in her trade. 'Our Pike deserves retirement and a quiet old age, poor thing, after eighteen years' hard work. Nowadays, all he's good for is to trundle along in front of a wagon at half a useful pace.' She grunted. 'And that goes for his lordship, as well.'

Pell smiled.

'Will you take tea with us?' Without waiting for an answer, Mrs Bewes poured out into delicate china cups, as genteel as if she were sitting in a velvet chair in her own gracious parlour. She removed a small leather bottle from her apron, tipping its contents into her own teacup, and Pell caught a whiff of gin and peppermint.

The cup she passed to Pell smelled only of tea.

Mr Bewes explained that he was hoping to accomplish his business and set off for home as soon as possible. 'I'm too old for this,' he said, and Pell understood. The atmosphere of the fair, equal parts thrill and menace, offered the sort of excitement that sickened the soul. An excess of alcohol had so far made the crowd cheerful, but she knew it would not be long before the mood turned.

'I'll happily stay with the horses,' Pell offered, 'if you would like to look around with Mrs Bewes.'

Her offer was gratefully received, and Pell sat with Esther watching the comings and goings of the fair until finally the couple returned, and Mrs Bewes urged Pell to take a turn with her husband. 'The place is riddled with gypsies,' she whispered with a meaningful nod at Esther, 'and heaven knows what else. I think you'll find the protection of a man a blessing.'

Pell retrieved Bean from Esme, and set off with the old man. She would certainly find work here, she told herself. Horses needed grooming and guarding, and owners would not want to leave a wagon, or a beast, unattended.

The noise did not abate as evening closed in, rather the opposite, due to the combined effect of drink and high spirits. Everywhere fires burned; the wood smoke blew around Pell's head and up her nose, a welcome smell over that of ordure and blood. She could hear pipes and fiddles emerging here and there in the dusk. The smoky grey evening made a perfect dull foil for flames and the flickering glow of lanterns.

She saw Bean's eyes glow huge like beacons in the failing light. Plenty of ugliness to be found here, Pell thought, despite it lying low. And he's just the child to see it all. She folded his cold hand between her two and squeezed it tight.

Pell managed to follow Mr Bewes and discourage him once or twice from horses he'd regret buying. She offered guidance so subtle it made no particular impression on him, but when he settled on a big skewbald gelding, well built and sound, it was thanks to judgement other than his own. Even in the half-light she could tell that the animal was strong, intelligent enough and willing. As they turned to go, the owner swung Bean up on to his horse's back, saying, 'See? Quiet as a lamb he is. Wouldn't hurt a fly.' The big horse turned his placid brown eye on Bean and they held each other's gaze for a moment. And then Bean leaned forward and laid his cheek against the broad soft neck.

'There's your answer,' crowed the man. 'Boy knows a good horse when he sees one.'

Which was true enough.

10

They returned to find the gypsy caravan empty and Mrs Bewes crouched over her fire, stirring a pot of barley and bacon soup. She insisted Bean and Pell join them, and they ate together, Pell grateful for a hot meal and the luxury of meat. Mr Bewes snorted when Pell asked if they were missed at home.

'Six married children all with children of their own. That's more than enough souls to run the place into the ground perfectly well without us,' he said. 'And Mrs Bewes does enjoy having no one to please but herself.'

The lady in question adjusted her skirts and settled back comfortably to prove his point. 'If only I can prevent Mr Bewes from finding himself a suitable animal for at least a day or two, I might even have a chance to see the sights.'

The old couple retired to their wagon for the night and Pell lay beside Bean on a pile of sacks with Jack tethered close by. She felt comfortable enough but couldn't sleep, despite being tired. It was impossible to ignore the party that had begun nearby with a pair of fiddles and a Jew's harp, joined a few minutes later by a makeshift drum, pennywhistles and flutes. At first the songs were loud and wild, but after some time they turned melancholic. Eventually, in a haze of half-waking, half-remembered dreams, Pell slept.

She awoke later in the dark to the sound of a gruff burble of words, stern and low at first and then sweet as a lover's, and she wondered who might have settled behind them. The voice affected her oddly, its soft hypnotic flow insinuating itself into the space between sleep and wakefulness. With no face to put to the sound, she nonetheless felt the tug of it.

What remained of the night was restless. Men with too much drink in their bellies staggered into strange camps, attracted like moths to any lantern or campfire. Nearby, a stallion, smelling every mare on heat in the square mile, screamed and groaned *unnnh unnnh unnnh*, rearing up and thudding down with all his might. Those mares were answering him too, and the already volatile atmosphere thickened.

People began rumbling their annoyance, and a few shouted, '*Shut the beast up!*' But the trumpeting, groaning, thudding and chain-clanking went on, and Pell thought, Someone's got to do something about that horse. But nobody did, and for the rest of the night she lay awake.

In the early dawn, when the possibility of sleep had passed, she edged away from Bean and stoked up the fire for the kettle. Quite near to Jack, a man sat awake in the near-darkness nursing a smouldering fire and a pipe; when he spoke, Pell recognized the voice she'd heard in the night. A pair of shaggy deerhounds lay crouched at his feet like sphinxes, heads up, eyes alert. The man had black hair streaked with grey, and his eyes glittered blue-black and gold, reflecting the fire. When he spoke to his dogs, they turned their heads gravely to listen.

They were the only two people awake in the vicinity, though the entire town would soon begin to stir. When he turned and held her gaze, Pell shivered, unable to look away, knowing what

Mam would say about encouraging a strange man in a place like this. But he didn't change expression, just stared at her until his curiosity was satisfied and then turned away. When next she dared to look, he and the dogs were gone.

Mr Bewes rose and dressed, anxious to revisit his horse, while Mrs Bewes reminded him that their budget wasn't a penny over twenty pounds no matter what sort of animal he fell for, if he didn't want his family going hungry all winter. Her husband tipped his hat and was off, dodging a child dressed in nothing but a pair of his big brother's boots.

The sun came up strong and hot, and despite yesterday's rain, a thin curtain of dust hung in the air, rendering horses and men indistinct. Boys with great sacks of feed on their shoulders jostled each other as they called out to buyers, and it became difficult to push through the crowds. One man grabbed on to Jack's headstall and said, 'What're you asking for this one, girl?' and pointed to a bony-polled bay who might have had half a soup spoon of thoroughbred blood in his veins, and said she could have him for eighteen guineas and 'him worth more'n twice that'.

'Thank you, no,' Pell said politely, thinking, Anything I paid for that horse would be too much. She had already seen a fair few horses worth owning, but many more you couldn't have paid her to ride away.

All that day Pell sought work, and all that day heard nothing but rejection, often in the least flattering terms and sometimes accompanied by offers that had nothing to do with honest wages. The stables and liveries had legions of small boys to do their bidding. At the Coach and Horses she applied to help with grooming and mucking out, but the owner's wife said without any civility that they'd plenty of help and didn't need doing with a snake in the henhouse and her own bastard besides. Pell held Bean by the hand and took her leave with a careful dignity she didn't feel. For an hour or two, she joined a milling group hoping to find places as household staff, but the takers for workers without proper references were few and far between. At another hotel she offered to cook or clean or serve, but they were too busy even to reply. By late afternoon she had exhausted every possible avenue and thought bitterly that she might have better luck in the empty villages all those people had left behind.

Returning to camp, she found Esther's children gathered around Mr Bewes and his new horse. It was marked like a Friesian cow, with a broad honest chest and four good legs all around. The horse lowered his head and lipped the front of Bean's shirt, and the boy wrapped his arms round its nose and nuzzled its cheek, making chirping noises like a bird. The horse looked no worse in daylight than he had the night before, and Mr Bewes clucked to him and led him round in a circle.

'He's a beauty, ain't he?' said he, but Mrs Bewes wasn't pleased.

'What do you think of that man,' she complained loudly to Pell, 'wasting good money on a gypsy nag?' And she refused even to look at the horse.

Mr Bewes winked at Pell, but the couple was put out with one another. Mrs Bewes attempted to exact revenge by demanding that her husband purchase a pony for her favourite grandson, 'who's been begging for a horse of his own,' said she, 'since he could walk.'

'Foolish woman,' snorted her husband. 'All that talk of being careful with money, and then wanting six months' wages spending on a child.' He shook his head. 'Twenty-nine years we're married, and her determined to put me in the workhouse every one of them.'

Pell expressed her sympathy for him, and when the time came for them to leave she bade them farewell with a cordial smile, and they wished her luck finding a horse. But it was her own worsening situation that occupied her now.

At the Haunch of Venison tavern on the other side of Salisbury, her father – having considered the day too warm and the night too cool to search for runaway children – redoubled his ever-futile attempts to slake his thirst. He would tell his wife that they could not be found, which was close enough to the truth, for they could not be found by a man whose only view was of the back room of a drinking establishment.

It was not long before Joe Ridley experienced difficulty locating his own backside as well, and so he slept under a bench till dawn, satisfied that the price of half a dozen flagons of ale had saved him the cost of lodgings.

11

Pell emerged from the womb with a view of ponies on the green, some of which had a habit of wandering into the house in search of food or company. By the time she was old enough to run, she was charged with bringing the mares in from the heath to foal, not an easy task, for they were moody and unpredictable in that state. And it was the strangest sight to see the little girl with her own wild mane of hair leading a string of swollen mares out of the forest, and them tame as tame, or so you thought till you tried to take over the job yourself.

The traditional way of herding involved ropes and traps and wild chases, catching what you could by the tail and hauling it in, or galloping a handful of ponies round to where someone was waiting with a gate and hoping they didn't swerve before the chute. Stillbirths were common, but in the absence of anything better that's what was done.

Pell's method confounded them, but it worked, transforming the process to something altogether more peaceful, with a word of calm and a slim hand to change the direction of a breech or a stuck foreleg. And afterwards she cleaned and stroked them and muttered fondly to them so they would not grow up wild.

Finch's children could all ride and catch a pony before their fifth birthdays, and Pell and Frannie learned just the same. In an acre of bays and roans and greys, they never hesitated in knowing which belonged to whom, and the name and nature of each. The yearlings given into their care they taught to stand quietly and be led, while the two-year-olds learned to carry a child to the next village or haul a load of cabbages to market. Like the rest of the Finches, Pell watched and learned the way to shape a shoe to correct a bad stride or foster a good one and, as she grew, to hammer it on quick as any grown man. Unlike them, she could see through the skin of a horse, through the thick bony skull to its brain, or deep into its chest where resided the heart and soul. She could tell at a glance what a horse could do, or might do if asked nicely, and how to ask so that the answer was always yes.

The day Birdie's father took Pell on to work for pay was the day he found her sat backwards astride the very devil of a stallion, untameable, or so everyone said, braiding celandine and hound's tongue through his tail. Her own father only noticed that she was a girl, and thus had no aptitude for preaching.

By fifteen Pell knew the farrier's craft as well as any proper apprentice, despite the fact that neither of her parents cared a whit for animals or could tell a pit pony from the Godolphin Arabian. Birdie's father made a habit of watching her, while thinking what a useful daughter-in-law he'd be getting in time.

'You'll make a fine helper for my son, one day soon,' he told Pell on her seventeenth birthday, pleased as pleased.

This pronouncement surprised her. She had always assumed Birdie would make a fine helper for her. The genesis of this misunderstanding was simple enough: she could handle a horse better than he could, and anyone with eyes in his head knew this to be true. That it was not the natural order of things she chose not to acknowledge.

On Birdie's twentieth birthday, when he learned that his uncle had leased him ten acres of his own and a cottage besides, he ran to her shouting that they could be married at last. And in that moment, years of unacknowledged doubt transformed into a roiling mass of dread. When Birdie saw the look on her face, he had to sit down.

'Aren't you happy for us?'

'For you,' Pell said.

'For *us*,' replied Birdie, reaching out to her. But she ducked away from him and ran out into the forest calling for Jack. She came upon Birdie's mare, Maggs, who showed the usual friendliness, happily ignorant of goings on in the human realm. The mare followed along until Pell turned on her, impatient, and shooed her off, whistling for Jack and him taking his time answering. When he finally did bother, she swung up on his back and asked him to run. Maggs ran beside them for a dozen strides and then slowed, more interested in standing quietly in the sunshine than racing across the heath for no reason.

Jack ran, and the wind whipped Pell's face while the pulse in her neck pounded out fear at the decision she had nearly made. Her thoughts had no time to catch up or take in what she felt, and the tears flew out sideways when she admitted to herself that she could not go through with it. But how could she betray him? They would have to be married and she would have to make the best of it, despite the fist that squeezed her heart dry.

She practised what would happen when he found her, what she might say and how to make it credible to them both. And when she saw him far off on Maggs, she raced to him but at the last minute didn't stop. It reminded him of the game they played as children, one of them standing in the path and the other galloping full tilt, and neither wanting to be the one to jump aside. Only this time he didn't move, but stood with a puzzled expression on his face until the last second, and it wasn't Pell but Jack who flinched, thrown back almost on to his haunches, so that when she flew up on his neck and then slipped off, trembling, Birdie was there to catch her in his arms and hear the words she knew he wanted to hear.

'When shall we marry?' She could barely speak, but answered before he did, 'Today? Tomorrow?'

He smiled then, and forgave her instantly, used to her moods and tempers and, like a fool, ready to put them aside. 'We'll need to post the banns,' he said, 'and you'll need a new dress.'

She was fierce then. 'No. We'll do it now.'

And poor Birdie clasped her to his heart while she panted against him like an animal.

'You're wrong to marry that boy,' her mother said when at last Pell came home, half crazed with determination. 'You won't make him happy and God only knows what he'll make you. Leave him to a proper wife. Someone who'll make a home for him, like Lou.'

Abruptly Pell was calm. 'I'll make a proper wife for him. I swear.'

Her mother, who knew her a hundred times better than she knew herself and a thousand times better than the simple-hearted boy next door, shivered at the calm as much as at the storm. And she was right, for Pell was thinking, I shall bring him his tea and work myself to death by the time I am thirty bearing children and scrubbing floors and working in the fields digging turnips till my hands bleed and my back gives out and everyone urges me to keep on for just one more year, at which point I will die of exhaustion and the meagreness of my own life. I will love him and care for him, will never tell him to get his own tea, or sweep the ashes from the hearth or give birth to his own twelfth child himself.

All of the strength in her, all of the resolve and pride and power in her would surrender to him now, and for an instant she felt a kind of relief. He would care for her, provide for her today and every day for the rest of her life, as long as they both should live.

Pell's mam sat with her eldest daughter, the older woman's face stony with doubt. She was not a woman to believe untruths, no matter how fiercely uttered.

12

There was money to be made in Salisbury. There was money to be made holding horses for a penny. The blacksmith made money, the horse dealers and bread sellers made money during the day, and the pickpockets, thieves, prostitutes and gamblers made money after dark. But what job could Pell do, except to look at a horse and know it?

All around her men sealed deals while the sun rendered the scene harsh and flat in the midday glare, then set it afire at twilight. As darkness fell, a man sang a mournful tune while a handful of others kept time, but the smoke from the fire made Pell feel faint and she moved away. Bean, who usually followed without complaint, tugged at her sleeve unhappily.

'Not much more,' she murmured, and picked him up in her arms. He weighed little enough, but she was tired too. Wandering further, she saw an old man holding two identical brown geldings, and the buyer who examined them merely an outline in the sinking light. Behind him stood another man, one she recognized even as a silhouette, with the shaggy deerhounds at his side.

His dogs had a quality that made her think of stag hunts and kings. The male stood nearly motionless with his head up, ears pricked, nose rising and falling gently to pick up scents in the wind, while the bitch trembled. Pell didn't like the anxious feeling flowing off her. You couldn't say they were handsome dogs, with their broken fawn coats and long noses, but there was a certain nobility and a good deal of greyhound in them and when their owner turned and showed his profile she shivered, and wondered if there might not be a good deal of greyhound in him as well.

As she watched from the shadows, the first man checked over every inch of the brown cobs, felt their knees and examined their teeth, while the owner looked on, silent. He had pulled one slightly forward, and Pell knew he meant to sell that one, despite pretending the buyer should choose whichever he preferred and it made no difference to him.

'Not a grain of sand between them,' said the owner proudly. 'Ought to sell them as a pair, but seeing as you've got your heart set on just the one . . .'

The buyer hesitated and Pell stepped up close behind Dogman, indicating the horse standing at the front. 'Not that one.'

He turned just enough to see who she was. Nightfall had erased the detail of his face, but his eyes crackled with sparks.

She nodded at the horse standing back. 'That one.'

The owner caught the nod and made a spluttering noise. 'Nothing one's got the other hasn't. Better stick to something you know, *miss*.' He looked from her to Bean with a sneer.

Pell said nothing, held fast by the black-and-gold eyes. At last, with a great effort of will, she freed herself and left.

Later that night the two men reappeared, one leading the big gelding, the good one. Dogman crouched down at his fire, blew gently on it to ignite the smouldering embers and lit his pipe. The other man approached her. His voice was sharp. 'I'd give something to know what you saw between those two. They looked as like as sparrows to me.'

She didn't know him, and he hadn't thanked her either.

'Well?'

'If you'd bothered trotting them out,' she said at last, 'you'd have seen how weak the other was behind.'

The man frowned, his face all doubt. 'Weak?'

Pell looked past him. He could think what he liked.

'You're quite sure of your own opinions, miss . . .?'

Take it or leave it, she thought. There was nothing in it for her.

Dogman watched her face carefully, but Pell was looking at his hounds now, noticing for the first time that under the dense tawny coat his bitch had a full set of hanging teats. So that's why she looked anxious. Poor thing.

'Can you do that horse trick more than once?' The man again.

She bristled. 'Trick?'

'Can you spot a good horse in a crowd? Because, if you can, it'd be worth something to me.'

'How much?'

Behind his friend's back, Dogman grinned. The other man merely blinked.

'Well,' he said, regaining his composure, 'if you can choose half a dozen sound horses, one hundred guineas to spend, there'll be five pounds in it for you.'

The sum was far more than she would have dared ask, and Pell said nothing for a long moment, struggling against an urge to shout assent. 'All right,' she said at last, 'if you can bother telling me your name.'

'Harris,' he said, bowing with exaggerated politeness. 'Does that suit you?'

She looked straight into his eyes and tried to fathom him. And then she almost laughed, because the truth was she needed the money so badly it didn't matter whether she could trust him or not.

13

Day three saw wall-eyed horses stood up against walls and lame ones brushed and polished and posing stock-still. Bootblack found new uses on lopsided or unlucky markings, and if someone had a horse with two short legs on one side, you'd sure as sure find him standing square on the side of a hill. The obvious beasts had been sold; what remained was the dust thrown up by a thousand men and horses, enough to obscure any truth that lingered in the place. Day three was for sharp-witted sellers and sharp-eyed buyers, and not a man in the place didn't fancy himself one or the other.

Esther had done whatever business she had come to do, taken the money, and disappeared. The children scattered through the fair seeking food and entertainment. Pell's father was long gone, encouraged on his way by an unpaid hostler. Meanwhile, Pell searched the crowd for Harris, and just when she began to think he must have changed his mind, he appeared.

'Let's go,' was all he said by way of a greeting, and off they set – Harris, followed by Pell with Bean last, trotting to keep up. Harris led them first to a handsome bay with a look in its eye that made Pell shrink. When she shook her head, Harris muttered to himself in a low voice, 'But does she know what she's about, eh?'

After looking at another two or three that he fancied, Pell said simply, 'I'll do the choosing from now on.'

It was an impossible arena in which to make decisions, and though she had no trouble picking a clean sane horse out of a herd scattered through a forest, she felt the strain of doing the same here. The place held so many people playing at smoke and mirrors and so many sizes and types of misfit men and animals that she could easily begin to doubt the evidence of her own eyes. But, thinking of the money, she squinted and watched, and eventually found a pretty little blue roan mare, delicately built and well put together, and she knew immediately from the look of her that to ride her would be a pleasure. And besides she was clean and healthy and had only not been bought because of her colour.

'That one,' she said, and the man who owned her said, 'The lady's got taste, sir.' Which is what they all said when you wanted to see one of their horses. He trotted her up and down, and sure enough she was a pretty mover with a temper to match. Harris bargained hard with the owner and got her for a good price. They led her away and she walked at Pell's side sweet and light as a doe.

It was nearly an hour before she saw another animal worth taking seriously, a piebald gypsy half-shire this time, broad and well-muscled with a nice willing manner and a kind eye. Except for people like Mr Bewes, who bought horses solely on the basis of work worth, the fashion wasn't much for a coloured pony, especially one that looked to have been painted by a drunk. But a well-shaped head, sound legs and a certain honesty attracted her. When Harris shook his head no, she ran her hand briefly down his neck and left a little sadly.

The next one she chose was a bony five-year-old gelding with a good deal of thoroughbred in him and a jagged blaze down his nose. He tossed his head and kicked out and the man who owned him seemed relieved to see him off for little more than he'd have got at the slaughterhouse. But bad treatment and not enough food can make any animal look ruined, and this one, Pell knew, had the makings of something better. When she felt his legs and stroked his face, he quietened right down, and she could tell from the length of his neck and the depth of his chest that once he was fed up and treated well, he'd be worth five times what they paid.

Two horses.

They made an offer on a black mare, but the owner turned them down, wanting a higher price. A rangy grey paced nervously on a short tether; he was bony and high at the withers, too big round the barrel, and stained green from living out. But having seen him move, she nodded. The same horse as he would look on good oats and exercise shone out at her, but she could not convince Harris.

And so the hours passed. It took all day to find six horses they both agreed on, and by the end of it Bean dragged his feet and Pell felt weary to the bone. Harris made fewer and fewer objections, but stood back and let her have what she liked, paying up each time while she silently kept track of the money and her cut of it. Occasionally he'd mark out a horse he thought looked good, and she'd point out a stiff hock or a bad way of moving, and sometimes she wouldn't bother but just shook her head and went on, and by the end of the day he'd learned a thing or two about choosing horses and she'd learned a thing or two about driving a bargain.

He tied all six horses in a string behind his own, and told her he'd deliver her cut of the money in an hour, after he'd finished with another piece of business at the inn. At first she objected, not trusting him to return, but he threw down his bag and said, 'That's everything I own but what I'm wearing.' And she didn't have much choice but to accept.

When an hour passed, and then two, and then more, the anxiety began to rise up in her. And it grew, and grew, until, not knowing what else to do, she left Jack with Bean, and ran through the town towards the inn to seek Harris and the horses. It took only ten minutes, but when she arrived, the innkeeper informed her that he'd paid up and gone.

With a sense of confusion she ran back to the place she'd left, to find nothing but an empty square of trampled earth where only moments ago there had been a child, and a horse. It was this desolate square of earth upon which, two frantic hours later, filthy, exhausted from searching and near-crazed with a sense of futility and the world's injustice, she collapsed.

14

Bean had long practice in watchfulness. He knew how to recognize danger by the expression on an unwary face and to judge how a situation might turn. So when Harris began to thread his way back through the crowd with his horses, Bean watched carefully to see what might happen next.

He watched the man dismount hurriedly, watched him cast about, bemused.

At last Harris approached him, reluctant to engage with the halfwit, but anxious to conclude his business and get on.

'Where's the girl gone?'

Bean pointed across the crowd and Harris followed the direction of his finger. Seeing nothing there of interest, he scanned the vicinity and exchanged a few words with a man nearby who only shrugged. After another minute, Bean saw the wheels in Harris's head begin to turn, saw a decision form in his brain.

The man turned to Bean, speaking in an exaggerated manner. *'Tell her. I waited. As long as. I could.'* And he laughed at the thought of the halfwit telling anyone anything. Then he reclaimed his bag, mounted his own horse, tightened the tie of the lead rope and rode away towards the far reaches of Salisbury Plain where he might disappear for a time.

What was Bean to do then? If he didn't act, all would be lost; the retreating crowds could be counted upon to hide any number of dishonest men leading strings of ill-gotten beasts.

His brain spun wildly as he searched the crowd for Pell. She must be nearly here, *she must be*. But she wasn't. So he scrambled up on Jack and followed the man who would take his sister's horses without paying for them.

Harris eschewed the obvious routes out of Salisbury, opting for a little-used cattle path that skirted the cathedral and disappeared almost at once into a wood. The path's obscurity made Bean's job difficult, but he kept well back, depending on the noise and trampled ground left by his quarry to mark the path.

His anxiety increased as they moved further and further from the centre of Salisbury. After one hour, then two, then three, he gave up hope of Pell catching them, and the decision he'd made in a moment of desperation suddenly filled him with doubt. Lost and frightened and hungry, it occurred to him that it might be beyond his power to right this particular wrong. More hours passed. He had no idea how to bring Harris to justice, no idea how to turn back and find his sister. The more time that passed between the original crime and the present moment, the more dismayed Bean felt, until he began to consider his task impossible and his original decision to follow Harris wrong.

For two days and nights, Harris travelled, stopping only for an hour or two at a time to sleep and rest the horses. And for two days and nights Bean followed him, increasingly exhausted and consumed with hunger so that he began to ride Jack by balance and momentum alone, his head drooping forward over the horse's neck, while Jack walked evenly and gently so as not to unseat his rider.

Jack harboured no thoughts of returning to his mistress. This indicated no particular shortage of imagination on his part, for a horse will generally behave unremarkably unless ill-treatment or lack of food persuades him to do otherwise. Did he think of Pell, or wonder at the fact that Bean had taken sole charge of their journey? Perhaps he did. But more likely he wondered at his rider's growing passivity, wondered when he would next be allowed to stop and eat or drink.

And so they plodded on, ever more slowly, until on the third night Bean slipped off and, tired as he was, malnourished and cold as he was, did not get up again but lay still on the ground, hugging his arms round his small thin body, half dazed and half unconscious, waiting for something to happen that would change his luck, while Harris and his horses disappeared into the night and Jack cropped grass beside him.

Of course luck can always be depended upon to change, and Bean's did just that within a very few hours. By the time the sun had half risen on the morning of the following day, he had been discovered by a minor parish councillor who picked him up, spoke to him softly and with sympathy, asked him who he was and whence he came and, receiving no answer, deemed him an idiot, took control of the horse that stood patiently nearby and freed himself of all responsibility for the vagrant child by carrying him over into the neighbouring town and depositing him at the entrance to the workhouse.

Such a fine-looking pony would be no good to the poor idiot child, the man told himself, whereas if he sold it to pay a debt he himself owed it would relieve him of a most onerous mental burden. Cheered by this thought, the man set off for home leading his serendipitous find and whistling a little tune, pleased with his luck and the way this unpromising day had turned out.

15

Pell's search began with determination but few clues. A white horse. A man with two dogs. A boy who didn't speak. A horse trader. Even as she described all that she had lost, she could feel the hopelessness of it. What she sought matched too many boys, horses, men and dogs to be of use. She searched every square inch of the fair, increasingly desperate, describing the child, the men, the crimes as she saw them (kidnapping, horse-stealing, breach of promise, thievery), and praying for information with all the fervour of a person who has not, a mere half hour earlier, believed in the utility of prayer.

The one person she did find was Esther. The woman appeared just as she had before, surrounded by her children. She scrutinized Pell's tear-stained face and the empty space where there had recently been a horse and a child, and grasped the turn of events at once, shaking her head at Pell's story and saying of the two men, 'They'll both be long gone. And neither wanting to be discovered.'

The gypsy woman almost laughed. She had found the child. But the child would not stay found.

It was the last day of the fair, and only the dregs of society remained. Harris and Dogman might never have existed for all anyone recognized their names or expressed an interest in them.

The men she questioned all looked at Pell, putting together stories in their heads about her. It was none of anyone's business what she was after and why, but that didn't stop them wondering. Most had seen women in just this state at the end of other fairs, and men happy to be away.

By midday, when most of the crowd had packed up and moved off, she had made no progress.

It was Esther who returned with information of a poacher 'up Pevesy way', whose description matched the man with the dogs. The information gave no specifics, but was more than nothing and would have to do. 'We'll travel that way with you,' Esther said, and told Elspeth to pack up the wagon, just as if her company had been formally requested. And so, with a great creaking of harness and clattering of wooden wheels, they set off.

Dozens of other travellers shared the road, most leading horses bought at the fair, and Pell questioned each with a voice that quavered and lost conviction with each new rejection. They climbed on to the beginnings of Salisbury Plain and, turning back, Pell could see church spires marking out every hamlet for miles around with handfuls of houses scattered about each, and paths running from one to the other like a child's game drawn with sticks in the dust.

A peculiar dark-grey ceiling of cloud covered the plain, underneath which ran an illuminated stripe of sky and the bright yellow-green of rolling grassland. As they travelled, Esther collected plants to dry and sell for remedies in little cloth bags. 'Dog's tail,' she muttered as she walked alongside the wagon, 'fescue, red clover, sneezewort, scabious, horseshoe vetch, cat's ear.' Evelina followed, picking her own bouquet of flowers, which she later abandoned in a basket to wilt.

Pell could see the mounds of barrows in the distance, and Esther warned her to remain vigilant against spirits of the dead that would arise and scramble up her legs, sliding over her waist, across her ribs and into the empty places in her womb and heart. Despite not believing in spirits, Pell couldn't chase away this fearful image, and all evening as they rode through the uncanny landscape she shuddered at the ghosts whose cold tongues lapped at her ankles, hissing and threatening and plucking at their hems. Esther gave each child a small bundle of mullein and white sage to ward off bogles and revenants.

The rolling plain seemed to stretch forever in all directions. They progressed slowly, for Esther's wagon was heavy and Moses showed no inclination to hurry up hills. As they rested on the top of one, they could see the ancient giant's ring far ahead, its massive stones toppled like building blocks. Pell stared at the weird arrangement of boulders and Esther swung out to the east, giving the ancient stone circle a wide berth, tying her skirts tight around her ankles as they passed. They hurried along, staying off the ground and keeping the children inside the wagon until they'd lost sight of the ring and the barrows surrounding it. Whatever their beliefs, neither woman would risk disturbing the dead.

Every so often, Esther made observations about what lay ahead on the road or what would happen if they turned here or cut across that meadow. 'Just beyond here is a baker,' she'd say, and place a few pennies into the grubby hand of one of the boys, who'd fly off across a golden swell of waving grass and grazing sheep and return with a loaf of excellent bread. She knew every byway and huddle of houses on the plain, down to a dangerous ditch or an old elm up ahead that would make a good stopping point.

Pell noticed that once or twice a day there would be someone she knew, either to nod at or talk to in her quick Romany, with much gesticulating up the road and down the road, pointing east or west or both. But they never invited Esther to share a meal, or their tea, or to set down and stay, and there was something in Esther's manner during these encounters that made Pell wonder, for the gypsies they passed on the road seemed to travel and camp together in sociable groups. Perhaps it had to do with the children's father, if there was one, for his name was never mentioned.

At every crossing of paths, Esther left scraps of cloth tied on tree branches or piles of sticks and stones. She did not discuss their significance, or for whom they were intended, and Pell did not presume to ask. Perhaps, Pell thought, this network of pointings and signs added up to some sort of map; perhaps the world surrounding Salisbury Plain existed intact in Esther's head, complete with every tree and hedge and fork in the road. This made Pell imagine her as an owl, floating silently over the countryside, aware of each stile, each fallen branch, each rut in the road, each mouse and shrew.

But she didn't know where to find Bean or Jack, which would have been a good deal more useful.

As they travelled along a quiet stretch of road, Esther turned to Pell and said, in a voice that assigned no importance to the question, 'Your father is a preacher?'

Pell nodded, baffled by the woman's ability to know things. 'Yes. A non-conformist man of God. From Nomansland. He lived with us only when no one would pay him to preach elsewhere.'

Esther turned away with a weird smile. 'I met a man like that once.'

'He is not the only one plying such a trade.'

'True.' And then, 'I hoped to meet that man again.'

Pell frowned. 'Most meet such men only when they cannot avoid it.'

'He wronged me,' she said. But did not elaborate further.

For a time they were both silent. Then Esther turned once more to Pell, with a slow smile. 'And you? You left home to seek your fortune?'

'I left home on my wedding day.'

The other woman threw her head back, cackling approval. Neither of them said anything more.

The midday meal was kettle broth made from hot water and bread with a bit of lard and a handful of grubby brambleberries. Esther stuffed tobacco into her clay pipe and puffed away, sipping her tea, while Pell took Evelina on to her lap and showed the little girl her book of birds. The child's eyes hardly dared blink, and it occurred to Pell that she had never seen a book before. In an atmosphere of near-religious awe, the child pointed to each bird, her finger hovering off the page, fearful of touching the pictures and silent with amazement. Pell told her the names, which Evelina spoke in Romany, along with the sound each made. Her favourite was a delicate pencil-and-watercolour sketch of a puffin, at the sight of which her eyes opened wide, astonished that such a bird – with its big bill and orange feet – existed.

Even after Pell put the book away the child remained stock still, staring at the place it had been, willing it to return, while Pell gazed at Evelina, willing the hard little face to take the place of the silent boy she'd lost.

Later, Pell found her squatted down, drawing her version of a puffin carefully in the dust with a twig, while the rest of the children gathered round hooting in disbelief. When she saw Pell watching, she stopped drawing and stared back with silent dignity, waiting for her to leave.

Esme, who had been eyeing Pell with a look of misery and outrage since they set off together, continued to glare at every encounter, as if Bean's disappearance indicated carelessness on Pell's part. She had a disconcerting way of stealing up silently when Pell least expected it, hissing a single question over and over: 'Where's Bean?'

Eammon and Errol had different games in mind, running off across the plain in search of things to eat. They disappeared so often and for such long stretches of time that no one seemed to notice their absences or find it surprising when they appeared now and again with a scrawny chicken or rabbit for the pot. Pell asked if Esther ever worried she might lose them, and she replied that if one or two children went missing there'd be more food for the rest. Nothing in her face indicated whether this was her version of a joke.

One evening, the boys turned up with a bag they'd half carried, half dragged from some distance away. Pell had disposed of her scruples and felt pleased at the thought of meat that night. But what they pulled out of the sack was wriggling and whining and glad as day to be free, with two pointed faces, a soft black-and-grey coat and a body swinging wildly in all directions attached to two wild sweeps of tail. Once separated, the beasts looked ugly as skinned rabbits, all ribs and bony legs and long straight feet, and just two more mouths to feed as far as Pell could see. When she asked the boys what their plans were, and could she put the pups in the pot for dinner, Eammon grinned, picked the male up by its scruff and handed it to her, saying, 'He's for you.'

Well, the problem with beasts is how they latch on to you with their eyes, and the skinnier the creature, the bigger and more determined the eyes. 'Take him back,' she told them, but they danced away and meanwhile the thing managed to scruffle its front half up on to her lap faster than she could push it off. She turned impatient with Eammon who just grinned and said, 'He likes you all right.'

What was left of her heart sank for being burdened yet again with attachment.

The next quarter hour was spent digging the animal out of her sleeve or from under her skirt or trying to untangle it from around her feet, and Pell thought it had probably been stolen and missed some person at its proper home.

But Esther looked at the pups dispassionately. They were not babies, but scrawny adolescents, old enough to have lost their needle-sharp teeth and endearing expressions. 'Whoever owned them didn't much care for them,' she said. Which was a sentiment there was no arguing with, especially once Eammon explained that they'd found the pups already nicely packaged in the sack with a large stone thrown in for good measure.

The rest of the little ones snatched them away and took them off to worry till the poor things cried for help and quiet, and there was nothing to do but claim them both back and feed them bits of bread till they curled up together, eyes closed and whimpering. Pell ate a meal not much better than the one she'd given them, and when the time came for bed, the children took the bitch and Pell pushed the dog away from her so it curled up tight in a miserable ball alone beside her on the cold ground. And finally, half asleep and wholly impatient, Pell pulled the shivering creature in beside her, where, with an almost human sigh of gratification, it placed its head against her heart, and went immediately to sleep.

Next day at dawn when she rose to light the fire, the animal followed exactly at her heel or under it. She looked down and, despite the appeal in his eyes, would surrender neither bread nor feeling. But Eammon and Errol saved her thinking about him further by whistling the pair off across the fields and almost before the tea had finished brewing and the breakfast been cleared they were back with three fat rabbits killed clean, and the creatures happy with a carcass to chew in addition to whatever scraps of skin and bone didn't go into the pot. After just a few good meals both animals looked less like ugly crows, and with rabbits in the pot Pell found herself accepting their presence more gratefully. Not that it mattered a whit whether she accepted them or not.

In daytime, the two would join the muddle of children at her feet until she drove them away, and at night the bitch was banished to a place underneath the wagon, while the dog waited till Pell was asleep and crept around silent as a thief so that next time she woke he'd be there, with his spine against the curve of her belly where she'd once kept Bean, and his head pressed as near as possible to the beating of her heart.

He didn't have a name at first, though the little ones called them Dicken and Dog. And despite Dog being a bitch, and despite Pell wanting to come up with something better the names stuck.

16

Pell's father's family were clergymen of the worst sort: charming, immoral and unkempt, with livings too small to keep a family and behaviour unbecoming men of God. Each generation spawned another more engaging and worthless than the last, capable of providing neither a living nor spiritual guidance, unless someone needed guiding to an inn. They had always tended towards the outer edges of religion, and Pell's father, educated to a point that made his position impossible in every social sphere, compounded the sins of his fathers by declaring himself a non-conformist, a Primitive Methodist with a firm belief in God's love for the poor and the weak. This, Pell considered a lucky coincidence, given the state of his finances and temper. As for her mother's family, what they lacked in fecklessness they made up for in a talent for hopeless marriages.

Pa's best quality was the fact that he was so often gone. His adventures out on the road were hidden from the family, but there were rumours, and one day he arrived home with a boy baby swaddled up tight in the shape of a bean, and turned the child over to Mam to bring up as her own. Pa never said whose baby it was, but the dark hair and huge eyes matched one or two of his other children well enough to raise certain conjectures.

Birdie's family were the other sort, the hard-working, honest, resourceful sort of family. He had a father, grandfather and great-grandfather, all with a lifelong dedication to livestock. It was Birdie's family who taught Pell everything she wasn't born knowing about animals, and it was Birdie who gave her Jack. Not that Jack was the sort of gift a person would receive gladly.

From the start he was an odd-looking creature, with big raw joints under his dull coat, and every bit of him awkward and badly attached, or so it seemed. His dam, a plain, bad-tempered thing with not much to recommend her, first failed to produce enough milk and then compounded the insult by losing patience and kicking him away. None of the other mares would have him.

Birdie's father was all for letting him die, not believing there'd be much use in him, but after a good deal of begging and bothering, he handed the foal over to Birdie, who handed him over to Pell. She recognized at once that he was more a burden of work than a gift, but she took pity on him, hauling him up on to her lap and dipping her fingers in mare's milk so he could suck. And eventually the poor thing got so displeased with her interference that he picked himself up, shook her off and drank from the bucket all on his own as if to say, *There, I hope you're happy now*.

It was her first hint that she'd been given something worth having.

For a time, they stabled him with a cross-eyed pony scarcely bigger than a dog, but it was Pell he thought was his mam. Birdie's dad shook his head at the two of them, thinking what a waste of time it was rearing the ugly thing. But he was a stubborn little nix with a magnet eye, and at the end of a year his coat had started to turn from dull black to grey, and against all expectation the bits that didn't fit looked to be joining up. At three he was pure white except for his muzzle and a black mark the size of a penny on his left flank. He had a big intelligent head, a thick arched neck, and gaits so sweeping and free, no one ever thought to wonder why she'd saved him. It was said that Arab horses had been bred to local ponies a century ago in an attempt to improve the breed, and once or twice every generation the Arab blood emerged. Even if you hadn't known about the rogue ancestor, you might have guessed by the size and the shape of him, so different did he look from the rest. It branded him superior and strange, all at once.

Pell began backing him as soon as he was strong enough to bear her weight, and he didn't act as if he minded, only at the beginning turned to look at the odd new thing. When he was three and a bit, they'd ride along the moors with Birdie and his mare, Maggs, just walking or jogging with a loose rein so he'd get used to the feel of her. Until one day Maggs flushed a brace of grouse by nearly stepping on them, and the noise and flapping startled her into a dead run with Birdie hanging on for dear life. Jack seemed to consider the situation before making up his mind to follow, and then off they went at a gallop. Pell imagined one of his legs down a rabbit hole while she died of a broken neck, but Jack seemed born knowing what to do with a field full of holes, and didn't ever put a foot where it oughtn't to be. And that was only one of his talents, for it was also the day she discovered he could fly.

For those poor souls who can only think of the terrible fear and danger of a runaway horse, think of this: a speed like water flowing over stone, a skimming sensation that hovers and dips while the world spins round and the wind drags your skin taut across your bones. You can close your eyes and lose yourself in the rhythm, because nothing you do or shout or wish for will happen until the running makes up its mind to stop. So you hold steady, balancing yourself in the wake, and unhook your mind from the everyday while you wait at the silent centre of it all and hope that the feeling won't stop till you're good and ready for life to be ordinary once more.

The problem being that she never was.

17

The gypsy children passed their time running and rolling and darting in and out of the horse's legs and bickering over anything edible. They took turns on Moses, who had feathered ankles and a steady, plodding stroll, balancing on him like circus acrobats though he took no notice of the flyweight creatures. When one child lost interest in riding, it would slide off and allow a different one to scramble up in its place. Their mother didn't interfere except with a look or a *hssst* to indicate danger. The activity and clamour of them distracted Pell from her troubles, for which she was grateful.

After another morning on the plain, they began to descend into a hilly vale and Esther stopped and said, 'Look.' Pell followed the direction of the gypsy woman's gaze, and for a moment her heart stood still in wonder. She had heard of such things, but never imagined that she would see one. It faced left with all four limbs straining outwards, its long curved neck thrown up across the hillside. It may once have been pure white, but now its outline bled into the surrounding hillside, and the graceful chalk body was dappled all over with flora, blurred, but with the clarity of its spirit intact.

'Legend says he once had a boy rider,' Esther mused. At this, Esme frowned, and glared at Pell, for there was no sign of the boy.

They might have stood all day just looking, but Esther slapped the reins, and Moses lifted his mighty head and walked on. For half a mile the white chalk horse stayed on their right, changing position as they moved around it, until eventually they entered a wood and it danced off without them.

By noon, the autumn sun had taken the chill off the day, and it was a beautiful evening when finally they left the main road. Esther stopped for a conversation with a small encampment of gypsies, then led her family on to a tiny twig of a path that opened into a quiet meadow, hidden from the road by a long stand of hedge. While Esther built a fire and boiled the kettle, Pell turned Moses out to graze, watching as he stood switching flies. With the white horse still skipping in her head, Pell brushed tears from her eyes with an impatient hand.

Elspeth fetched a china teapot and a stack of cups, holding the pot steady as Esther poured hot water over a handful of dried leaves.

'I have business to the south,' Esther said, 'so will accompany you no further.'

Pell's heart sank as Esther stirred her tea round and round, sipping it up through her front teeth with a hiss. That night Pell slept badly, dreaming of Nomansland.

The next morning, they came to a stone marker pointing towards Southampton in one direction and Pevesy in the other. Esther nodded goodbye to Pell, her eyes already on the next stretch of road. Circumstance had postponed her business for some years, she said, and she was impatient to get on.

The children crowded around Dicken, sad to see Dog's twin go his separate way.

'You can take him with you,' Pell told Eammon, who grinned

and tried to lure Dicken to follow the wagon, until Esther put an end to that plan and sent him scampering back.

'I hope you find the boy,' Esther said to Pell, but did not turn to look at her.

As they disappeared down the road, Esme threw a stone over her shoulder in a final gesture of good riddance, and only Dog and Evelina looked back with any degree of longing.

Pell gazed after them, utterly dejected. Alone, poor and shabby, on a fool's mission, she wondered for an instant if even Nomansland offered more solace than this.

Using nearly the last of her money, she bought a brown loaf, broke off a piece and spread it with rosemary and lard. Dicken's huge soft eyes projected such a picture of loyal, careworn amity, and in so beseeching a manner, that eventually she threw him a crust. But far from snatching it and swallowing it down, he delicately sniffed and picked it up carefully as if deciding which would be better, to starve or eat crusts. He was a funny old thing, grazing on weeds or whatever else he might find about the place, though it was with rabbits that his true passion lay. Pell would see him freeze, watching, ears pitched up, body rigid with excitement. And she would hold her breath and wait and wait and at the last moment whisper, '*Go!*' and he'd *go*, in a frantic chase of perfect joy. And although sometimes he won and sometimes the rabbit won, she never tired of watching.

Staying with Esther had reduced life to a series of prescribed choices. *That field there catches the morning sun. No one ever bothers with that barn. Half a mile from here we'll stop.* But Pell didn't know the route or whose field lay fallow at what time of year, or where there was a sunny clearing in a protected wood. Being a stranger, she would always be an object of suspicion, even without the gypsy dog at her side. She had to keep a sharp eye out for a place to sleep, and couldn't stop worrying till she'd found it; it didn't do for a single girl in the company of a flibbertigibbet with a guilty expression to be caught without shelter as night came.

In the evenings everyone would be out, the children playing games in the dust, hens scratching for grubs, cats prowling, women leaning over their front gates for gossip, men returning from work. When Pell passed through, they fell silent and watched, six or eight or ten pairs of eyes, until after she had greeted them and passed by with excruciating slowness, smiling a little if any happened to return her greeting, but otherwise looking neither left nor right. And then before she was even out of earshot the murmuring would begin, the conjecture on her dress, her origins, the theory of who she was and why a girl *like that* was abroad, alone, far from home, leading such a dog, *and at this time of night*. Even if they remained silent, she could read their thoughts as clearly as if they had spoken out loud, for she'd lived her whole life in such a place. As for Dicken, there was little for him but stones and curses, despite his good nature and talent for friendship.

Tonight, she stopped by one garden gate to ask a young woman if she might exchange a fat rabbit for fruit from her orchard, and the result was an apron full of sweet hard pears, a thick slice of cheese, and another of bread and butter.

Pell reached down to thank Dicken, and he took the opportunity to pluck a pear gently from her pocket and retire to the side of the road, out of reach, to gnaw upon it.

She tossed a pebble at him, and he looked up at her, affronted, before returning to his pear.

They walked on.

18

At the edge of the New Forest, Moses shifted his weight off one huge hoof and sighed contentedly. How many times had Esther guided him back across Salisbury Plain, plying whatever trade she had chosen that week for feeding her children? Such joy to stop here on a cool autumn evening, standing ankle deep in grass while the world around him slowly filled up with dark. The wild shouts and giggles of Esther's children rose and fell in fierce cadence across the meadow, until night fell and one by one they clambered into the wagon, settled and fell quiet. Anyone passing would have imagined the world silent, except for the harrumph of a drowsy horse or a restless child.

For those few hours, the children were alone. Esther had unfinished business a few miles away in Nomansland with regard to two grievous crimes. For nearly a decade she had been unable to avenge herself of these crimes, and satisfaction might have continued to evade her had she not recognized a long-lost relation at Salisbury fair.

She set out to renew her acquaintance.

The inn she sought occupied an uncomfortable position on the edge of Nomansland, neither here nor there, split in half with its front door in Hampshire and its rear in Wiltshire. It was not at all usual for a woman to enter the place, and even less usual for a woman such as Esther, and so she stood outside and waited, and waited, and at last had enough of waiting. A handful of men looked up as she entered, their faces hostile, wondering at her business there. He did not recognize her at first.

'Am I so changed?' asked she, with her hard, crooked smile. 'You are not.'

'Time alters us all,' the man mumbled, rising uneasily from his place by the fire.

She held him with her gaze. 'Some more than others. A babe, for instance. So that his own mother might barely know him.'

The man's eyes flew open, and he staggered a little, then fled the inn with the woman close behind. He stopped in a place where they might not be overheard, straightened himself and mustered the voice calculated to overawe his parishioners. 'Would you have had me abandon the child to a life devoid of Christian virtue?'

Esther shrugged. 'He was conceived well enough without it.'

'But a Christian child,' the preacher stammered, 'required a Christian family to raise him.'

The appeal met no sympathy. 'You pledged a sum of money for that privilege.'

'I did, yes, but times were difficult . . .'

'Difficult?' Esther's impassive eyes flared. 'Did I ask for a sixth child? You were welcome to the bastard, *on the terms we agreed*. But I received no such terms. And in the meanwhile, my own five have near starved, year after year, rejected by the father that conceived *them*. He believed the fiction you told, that the child was conceived in desire. *That I was willing.*'

Ridley cast about, like a hare for a thicket. 'What do you want? I have no money, and the boy is gone.' And then he began to mutter something about God and His ways, but she stepped closer and spat in his face, her mouth twisted with a terrible intensity of loathing.

'*No religion I have is as godless as yours.*'

The preacher reeled as if from a physical blow, then beat an unsteady retreat – unsteady from an excess of shock or alcohol, or perhaps both. Esther followed him at a distance, watched him enter his house, then sat for some time, invisible in a stand of trees, watching and smoking her pipe. She had waited patiently for the child to leave the family. It might have taken ten years more, or twenty. But no matter. Her plan had not required haste.

She saw an older girl and three younger leave the cottage in the quickening dark to fetch water from the well, and heard a snoring from within that sounded to her like the rattle in the chest of a man about to die.

Somewhat later, having accomplished in Nomansland what she had set out to do, Esther returned to her children, setting off early the following morning with all due speed across Salisbury Plain. By nightfall, they had reached a large estate with a secluded orchard in which she and her family had often, in years past, spent the night in peace.

From their camp among the apple trees, the children crept down across a series of rolling lawns to catch a glimpse of Lord Hayward's grand stables, in which sixty horses were attended by an army of smartly attired grooms. Had they managed to gain entrance to the stables and not been shooed away with stern threats and warnings, had they managed to trawl up and down the endless immaculate aisles of covetable horses, they might have come across a stocky white part-Arab, recently acquired under somewhat unusual circumstances for George Hayward's daughter, Caroline.

19

Pell felt a chill as they left the village, and hugged her shawl tightly round her shoulders, hurrying along a road thrown into shadow by a tall brick wall. At the first opportunity, she ducked through a doorway in its long blank length, hoping to find a place to sleep. Inside, the wall still held heat from the setting sun.

With Dicken close at heel, she walked quickly, on constant watch for someone who might object to their presence. Far across the gardens and fields she could see a grandly proportioned old farmhouse, constructed in a strange mishmash of Gothic arches and peaked roofs. Even from afar, the place had an abandoned air; whatever staff remained to keep house for the absent owner was nowhere in evidence. Dismissed, she thought, or perhaps just gone to earn money elsewhere.

She followed the wall until she came to the first of a series of garden rooms held in its curve. Ducking through a low arch, she skirted the unchecked growth of deep borders and flowers gone to seed, came to a second room, then a third and a fourth until finally she entered a kitchen garden that looked as if it had received somewhat more attention. The only light left now was in the sky, and Pell could just make out vast cabbages, beans twisted around long stakes as high as her forehead, the luxuriant feathery growth of fennel. Along the warm west wall, she saw the dark outline of espaliered fruit trees, heavy with apples and pears but unpruned, with branches reaching out into the garden as if overjoyed to be released from symmetry. She tugged at the top of a carrot and pulled out a gnarled giant nearly as long as her forearm, planted last year and left to grow unchecked for months. Jack will love this, she thought, forgetting.

Still no shelter. But the kitchen garden felt unnaturally warm and, frowning, Pell pressed her hands against the high south wall. It was too hot merely to have absorbed the heat of the day, and as she followed it further, she came to a huge hearth built into the wall, smouldering with the remains of a great fire. She had seen such constructions before: hollow channels conducting heat through the walls to raise the temperature of the gardens. The wall would retain its warmth for several hours after the fire died and, as the cold seeped into her bones, Pell felt the old temptation to curl up against warm bricks for the night.

There had to be a potting shed or other shelter nearby, she thought, a little panicky now with darkness upon her. No moon lit the sky, and she had to feel her way forward beside the wall, stepping over the tangle of plants at her feet. And then suddenly the wall gave way to another hearth, empty this time, and she crouched down inside it, peering along its dark hollow channels. The heat from the fire had been drifting through all day and the recess was as cosy as a badger's sett, though not noticeably cleaner. Outside, the temperature continued to drop. If only she could crawl into the wall a little way for shelter, she might be hidden for a time, and warm.

With Dicken whining at the base of the tunnel, she hauled herself up and wriggled in as far as she could go, edging forward along the gentle slope. Inside was narrow and sooty, but dry, smelling of smoke and earth and the thick musk of creatures. Even her dull human nose could discern the separate odours of fox, badger and rat; she was obviously not the first creature to take refuge here on a cold night. She pulled herself in further to where the conduit widened slightly and found that it made a moderately comfortable bed. Here, she curled up, her shoulders and hips resting on a crumbly layer of leaves and grass dragged in by previous inhabitants. She arranged her shawl to protect against the worst of the soot, despite a despairing sense that every inch of her was already blackened and smudged.

She called Dicken, who stood whining, unwilling to follow. At last he gave in and scrambled up the passage, pouring himself into the knife blade's space between his mistress and the wall, snuffling and whimpering with excitement at the musky smell of prey. Pell grabbed him by his scruff and held tight, frightened he might try to crawl up through the narrow passages and be unable to turn back. He protested in a voice clear as a child's, but eventually stopped struggling. Seduced by the delicious warmth and Pell's proximity, he lay calm in the velvety black.

The heat soothed Pell's ragged spirit and gradually she slipped into a doze, imagining herself hibernating, rolled up snug against the winter. She thought of home, of nights with a sister pressing on each side for warmth. And, like that, she slept well.

Dicken woke early, growling a warning noise deep in his throat as he struggled to turn round in the tight space. Peering down towards her feet, Pell could make out a figure crouched in the doorway, blocking the feeble light. The feeling of being trapped, gone to ground and kept there, was a bad one; the smell of fox and badger now telegraphed fear. She wriggled back through the semi-dark of the passageway, dragging Dicken behind her, and dropped awkwardly into the fireplace, nearly knocking the figure off its feet.

'*Lord Almighty!*' he shouted, leaping sideways in terror.

She saw it was a boy, dressed in short woollen trousers and a linen smock. He had a broad face, blunt features and bare feet, and in his arms carried a great bundle of sticks.

'I'm sorry to have frightened you.' Pell straightened herself. Soot streaked her clothes and left long black smudges on her exposed skin. Bits of brush and burrs stuck to her clothing, sticks and crushed leaves dropped from her hair, and the boy goggled at her, astonished.

'What are you?' He spoke slowly, his face white with shock, his accent thick as porridge.

'My name is Pell,' she replied sweetly, amused. 'And I beg your pardon, but I slept in the wall.' She smiled, aware of the picture she made, hoping he wouldn't raise an alarm.

'Are you . . . a person?'

'Of course I'm a person,' she said. 'What else would I be?'

'I dunno, miss! Why would a person sleep in the wall?'

Pell shrugged. 'One has to sleep somewhere.'

'But I'm about to light the fires. You might have been burned to death!'

'I wasn't, though.'

He didn't answer right away, but looked behind him. 'It's a dangerous place to sleep, miss. Because of the fire. And Mr Pottle don't much like people hanging about. Especially those that aren't supposed to be here.'

'I'll go, then. Only . . . I'm looking for a child,' she said. 'And a horse.'

The boy stared at her, aghast. '*In the wall?*'

'No,' she answered soberly. 'They were kidnapped. By a man who stole my money.' She smoothed her skirt. Her shoulder ached from where it had been wedged up against the brick all night and her legs felt stiff. If only she had a clean apron, and not last week's turned over to the less soiled side, now covered in soot.

'That's a sad tale, miss,' the boy said, looking over her shoulder and only half listening now. 'And excuse my being rude, but you really must go now. Come quick, before Mr Pottle gets wind of what's happened. I'll lead you out by the shortest route.'

He ran ahead sideways, awkward with his bundle of kindling, turning back every step to urge them on faster. Pell and Dicken tripped along at his heel, the latter stopping every few strides to sniff and leave his mark.

'Excuse me, miss,' said the boy, whispering loudly as he ran, 'but are you travelling on your own?'

'Except for my dog.'

'Yes,' he said, his face half hidden. 'Only . . . I wondered . . .'

'Wondered?'

'A girl like you. It makes no sense.'

'I have no one else.'

He stopped, horrified. 'But . . . where will you go?'

'To Pevesy. There's a man there –'

His face lit up. 'But, miss! I'm from Pevesy. My brother lives there still, with my mother.'

'I'm searching for a man with two dogs. A poacher.' Her heart sank at the description. It was worse than useless.

The boy looked sceptical. 'You could ask him, ask my brother that is. The smithy's boy.' From the distant lawn of the big house, Pell could see an ancient bowlegged man with a wheelbarrow approaching at considerable speed. The boy followed her glance, squeaked, 'Mr Pottle!' and was off again, away from her this time, the bundle of sticks flying in every direction.

'Wait!' Pell called after him. 'What's your brother's name?'

'Robert! Robert Ames!'

From the road, she waved at his retreating figure, and then set off. She didn't stop until they had rounded the next wide curve in the road and, looking back, could see nothing familiar.

20

All that cool morning she walked steadily uphill, sweating with exertion, then shivering as the moisture cooled in her clothing. If the walking hadn't been so strenuous, she might have enjoyed the views more, the great rolling swards of chalk grassland stretching out in all directions, skies dotted with hobby and merlin, circling, anxious to be off south. They passed scrabbly stands of juniper that led down to scarp lowlands, but the descent only signalled more climbing ahead. At last, from high on yet another hill, Pell spotted the tower of Pevesy church far below in the town. She didn't dare descend looking as they looked.

They found a wooden shed shielded from the road, its roof intact. Bread and watery beer made her evening meal while Dicken, ribs barely concealed by his soft winter undercoat, gnawed at the carcass of something that might have been a rat. When he came to her, she wrapped her hand round his muzzle and shook it gently, and he looked into her eyes and hummed his devotion to her in a low voice. Pell spread out half a bale of dirty straw and burrowed into it, hugging Dicken to her for warmth, but still the night-time hours passed slowly.

They rose before sun-up, Dicken reluctant, unrolling himself with a deep low stretch and a question aimed at Pell about his breakfast. Mist hung in the grey light all around them. A damp handkerchief would do for her toilette; rubbing it across her face and hands it came up black with yesterday's soot. It was some time before her skin scrubbed up clean. While Pell combed and plaited her hair, the sun rose above the horizon and her spirits rose with it. Despite the chill, she removed her filthy apron and checked the little cloth purse at her waist, knowing exactly what she would find there. Enough for bread for another day or two, no more, and then what would she do?

They entered town, curling down a steep hill and crossing over the Avon on a narrow wooden bridge. At the baker in Pevesy she bought yesterday's stale loaf, hard halfway through, though this didn't deter Dicken who grinned happily and carried his crust off out of sight before swallowing it down. The meal did little for the emptiness at the core of her. At home there was bacon only rarely, but they'd an orchard and a cow, and she dreamed of stewed winter apples with cream.

Past the chequerboard flint shops and houses, past a tall white mill already buzzing with activity, she smelled and heard the blacksmith's shop – the rusty tang of hot iron, the exhaling whoosh of the fire, the dark clang of hammers and hissing bellows – before she reached it. Pell slipped into the grimy interior, standing out of sight in a dark corner while her chilled limbs unfurled in the heat of the forge and she inhaled the familiar smoky combination of charcoal and sweat with something like bliss. A broad-shouldered young man with a thick leather apron and a blackened face peered at her from behind the left hind foot of a heavy carthorse. She'd seen his features before, only softer, less defined.

'Hello?' he said, wondering at her presence in this place.

'You wouldn't be Robert Ames?' And at his nod she said, 'Your brother told me where to find you.' She felt suddenly shy.

The young man frowned. 'Which brother? I've dozens.'

If she'd only asked the boy's name! 'The gardener's lad at the big house just along . . .' She pointed, flustered.

He winked at her. 'I haven't really got dozens. What help did he offer?'

She told him of her search, straining to be heard over the roar of the forge and hammer, as he finished fixing a high-ridged ploughing shoe to the great hoof. For a moment he disappeared in a shower of sparks.

'Come outside,' the young man said at last, releasing the animal's foot. Together they stepped into the farrier's yard where a number of horses stood tethered side by side, exhaling steam and patiently awaiting a turn. 'I don't know anybody by that name, and the other man, with dogs . . .' He frowned, shrugged and shook his head. 'You're sure Pevesy is the right place?'

She was sure of nothing.

'I'm sorry,' he said.

'So am I.' She might have cried.

'Don't mind my asking, but what is it you'll do now?'

Pell sighed. 'I shall need to find work.'

'What sort of work?'

She paused. 'I'm good with horses.'

'So am I,' he laughed. 'Would you put me out of a job?'

'Only if I could, Mr Ames,' said she, and smiled at him.

'We'll ask my mother. If you'll hold off till dinnertime, you can come home with me.'

Until then she made herself scarce, not wanting to inconvenience him. At midday, the young man led Pell and Dicken through the Pevesy streets at a brisk walk, till they reached a blue door with a small white horse painted on it. Pell stooped to examine it.

'My father painted it,' Robert said, 'after the horse on the hill. It's meant to bring luck.'

She'd take what was going, Pell thought.

Despite the bright day, the tiny house was dark inside, the table spread with a plain cloth on which was set bread, cheese, butter and ham with a jug of beer. Robert Ames introduced her to his mother, explained that she was looking for a man by the name of Harris, or a poacher with dogs, who had stolen from her. Pell noticed that he didn't explain her search further, adding only, 'She knows our Michael.'

The woman's face, pinched and suspicious, didn't alter at either reference. *Stole what from you?* her expression said. She stared hard at Pell, and when Robert left the room a few minutes later, she leaned in and spoke in a low, flat voice. 'He's to be married,' she said, 'and soon.' The rest was obvious: *So don't be getting ideas about him.*

Pell perched on the edge of a hard wooden chair, poised to leap up and flee. Dicken sidled up next to her.

'*He* can stay outside,' growled the woman, swatting at him. But a minute later when Robert returned, Dicken slid under the table next to an old collie, making himself invisible in the shadows. As Pell tucked gratefully into bread and butter and ham, she could feel Dicken's stare, and sighing, reached under the table with a chunk of fatty meat. A minute later, the dog stood up, wriggled round to Robert Ames' knee and laid his head on the boy's thigh.

'You won't be getting my lunch that way,' Robert said, pulling one of the silky ears.

'I will not have you feeding that animal,' hissed his mother 'Whssst!' She aimed her broom at the dog. 'Get out like I told you!'

Dicken scarpered and Pell looked away, ashamed.

'My aunt always needs extra help in the dairy,' Robert told Pell, and his mother frowned. 'I'll ask if she'll take you on for a bit. You could board there, for now.'

Pell nodded, counting the time since Bean and Jack had disappeared. Five days. Five days that felt more like a lifetime, and no idea what to do or where to go next. She would take a job if it were offered, for now at least, and first solve the problem of having no money. In the meantime, anything might happen. People heard things, or were seen. Children reappeared or sent messages. Horses found their way home.

Despite a tendency towards despair, she remained unable to imagine that she would not soon be reunited with all that she had lost.

21

Bean's clothes were taken away and the workhouse matron scrubbed him with cold water and soap made of lye and soda, which hurt his skin.

'He's not right in the head,' she told the girl who passed over the large jug of water. 'Just looks and looks at you like that. Infuriating, it is.'

'P'raps he can't hear.'

'Oh, he can hear, all right. And he can talk, I reckon, just don't fancy it. DO YOU, BOY?'

The girl peered at the huge moon eyes, saw them blinking rapidly to push back tears. 'He's not yet ten,' she said, 'but his face is rather like an old man's.'

'An old idiot's, more like. Not right in the head, like I said.' She turned her attention to Bean, shouting close up in his ear, 'ALL THROUGH NOW, IDIOT!'

Bean stared at her.

'See what I mean? He hears, he just don't act.' She laughed an unpleasant laugh, and tossed him a small pile of clothing. 'HERE, IMBECILE! PUT THESE ON.'

The girl took pity on him and picked up the clothes, handing them gently to the shivering boy. 'Take 'em, there's a good boy. They'll warm you up now.'

Bean accepted the awful clothes with trembling hands and, crouching down, began dragging the rough wool over his limbs.

'He's just the sort of brat I mean when I say certain of 'em shouldn't be allowed to live. Just a burden on the rest of us. And what caused him to be that way?' She leaned in close to Bean again. 'YER MOTHER HAVE LOOSE MORALS, DID SHE? DID YE KNOW WHO YER DAD WAS?' She turned to the girl. 'See? He don't even know who his dad was. Bet his mam didn't neither. Lower than animals, that sort of folk. Should be smothered at birth.'

The girl gasped. 'You mustn't talk that way! He's one of God's creatures.'

'So says the likes of you.' Matron sniffed. 'But God can't help what's thrown his way, whereas God-fearing folk can.'

One last time, the girl tried. 'His clothes aren't so bad. Someone took a care with them.'

'Probably stole 'em.' And with that, Matron folded her arms and closed the conversation. She had noticed the quality of his clothes, and would sell them on when she could.

Bean finished dressing and stood, head bowed, his hands clasped in front of him like a penitent.

'Come along now, we'll take you to your dormitory,' said the girl, offering him her hand, but Matron stepped up and snatched him by his hair, dragging him out of the room behind her. She was a big woman, and the child she dragged weighed practically nothing.

'Ugh! This'll have to go,' she said, giving his hair an extra tug for good measure. 'Probably crawling with vermin.' The three made their way down a long, cold corridor, Bean scurrying sideways to keep ahead of the huge raw hand dragging at him. At the end, they stopped. Matron opened a door, and shoved Bean in with her foot. 'That bed's empty,' she said, pointing to a sack near the centre of the room. 'EMPTY, DO YOU HEAR? You can stuff it yourself if it's not comfortable enough for you.' She slammed the door behind her, muttering about the undeserving poor, and how the master had the right idea in his running of the place, showing exactly what laziness brought in terms of wages.

Bean sat alone in the miserable room, trembling with unhappiness. He had no possessions, not even the clothes he'd arrived in, and despite the fact that his old clothes had not been recently washed, the quality of the wool and their careful construction had made them soft and comfortable on his skin. There was no hope that he'd find straw to stuff his bed, for the door was locked and the room's only window far too high for him to reach. All alone for the first time in his life, without family or sister or anything familiar on which to rest his frightened eyes, he withdrew inside his head and curled up into the smallest ball he could make of himself, willing invisibility, wishing for warmth, hoping for kindness, praying for deliverance. None of which arrived.

22

Bean's decision to leave Nomansland with Pell on the morning of her wedding could not easily have been predicted, for Mam doted on him despite his not being her child. From the time he was a babe, she could see straight through his pale skin to the blood pumping in tiny vessels below, and his legs never grew thicker, nor straighter, than twigs. She feared for his health, slipping extras his way when she could.

'The son of a poor unfortunate,' Pell's father had said on the day he turned up with the child. When his wife asked more about the woman, he explained it as a question of penury and paganism, a doubly sad case, and Pell's mam wondered how much poorer than herself a woman would have to be before she began giving her children away.

Despite all manner of unanswered questions she made a deal with her husband that night, accepting the baby on the condition that it would be her last. It was not in her husband's nature to accept such terms, but he had resources other than his wife to fall back on, and so he agreed.

With a new baby in the house such a usual occurrence, no one much noticed that Bean didn't actually belong to them. From the beginning, Mam set him on her lap and sang to him while she worked, as she'd done with each of the previous nine. The sight of her gnarled, misshapen fingers against the baby's smooth cheek made Pell look away.

The illness came to Nomansland via the usual route: London to Bournemouth on the coach, and then the slow, inexorable spread north and west, as cheerful carriers of fevers and plague travelled from village to village, selling trinkets, or household goods, or fish, or butchered meat to ladies who leaned in to catch every word of gossip from villages beyond their own, and caught every spray of spittle in the bargain.

First came the fever, the aches in the joints, and the cold which nothing could stop, then the burning that spread to arms and legs like a fire sweeping a field, and finally a fathomless cough that wracked the entire body until it broke apart. George was the first to fall ill and – though nursed day and night by Lou and Mam – died having passed the malady on to his bed mates in the order that they lay: first James, then John and finally Edward, sweet Ned, lying quiet and afraid, not wanting to be a bother, or to die.

Mam turned frantic and brittle, keening to herself in a way that made Bean cower, hands on ears, knees tucked under his chin. Each of her children's deaths came as a physical blow, hammering her into the ground so that she lost height and emerged shrunken.

Whatever killed the boys ignored the girl children altogether. After Ned died, they sat numb and motionless, waiting for the disease to cross over and attack the others. But it never did. Bean still slept in the house, while the girls (dressed in rough linen and woollen dresses with just a single shawl among them) stayed out of doors all winter and came home each day rosy with health. To the neighbours it looked like carelessness to lose four boys and keep the girls, that weren't worth half so much alive. For Mam, it was first the loss, then the disapproval of the loss that ruined her; the sense, somehow, that a lack of fastidiousness in blacking the stove might have caused her boys to slip away. No one much counted Bean as consolation, what with his silence and his odd ways. Behind her back they called him the cuckoo in the nest.

The village carpenter was so old he ought to have been hard at work on his own coffin. Unable to keep up with so many dead children, he enlisted Pa to hammer boxes together for the two younger – one for John and the smallest for Ned, both without a single right angle. Pell hated it. She imagined a shoddy coffin could hinder a person's access to whatever heaven there might be, cause him to overshoot somehow, or fall out and plummet back to earth in flames.

For the funerals, Pa claimed precedence over the vicar of Lover, and once established in the church pulpit refused to give it up. 'These innocents,' he began, 'shall be saved, and gathered up to the kingdom of heaven by His mercy. Yet here, today, before Him, stand sinners doomed to plunge downwards, down to the darkest circle of hell, where ye shall find rivers of flame to melt the very flesh off thy bones, accompanied by the terrible screams of a thousand lost souls. Repent!' By now he had begun to shake with self-righteous ire. 'Repent, O ye sinners, lest the devil scourge ye till his lash runs crimson with thy blood and though thou beggeth for mercy, it shall not be forthcoming. Repent, lest he pour red-hot lava over the filthy tools of thy fornication, lest he run through thee with his fiery pokers. And *then* shall ye think to repent, too late!'

Crucially, he seemed to have forgotten that the majority of souls gathered in the church that day were members of his immediate family, for whom sorrow and loss and overwork had relevance, and poverty, and rage against the vagaries of fate. But fornication?

Louder and longer he preached, calling for flames and trumpets and angels and demons to behave in ways that (to Pell) seemed unlikely in so unprepossessing a setting as Nomansland, and for the wrath of God and the punishments of Satan to be visited upon them all with an unseemly range of sadistic reproofs.

Mam acknowledged none of the many words he spoke, but sat looking straight ahead with empty eyes, and gained no solace from his sermon. When the hymns began, accompanied by exhortations and shouting, Pell slipped out.

The doctor from town declared the problem to be typhus. Not that he'd come out to visit the family when it might have helped, but four deaths in close proximity required official inspection against the possibility of epidemic.

'Definitely typhus,' he told Mam, looking down his nose at them all, and Pell supposed they must have looked filthy to him, despite being as clean as their existence allowed. It was no use blaming Mam, who walked on earth like something inanimate come partway to life.

The doctor required the bedding to be burned, which was no bother, it being straw. He also insisted that they fill in the night closet and dig it anew, and that the house be scrubbed top to bottom. And then he departed in his smart gig, hoping never to be summoned to such a place again.

These jobs fell to the girls. Despite the futility of scrubbing packed earth, thatch and sod, Pell and Lou attempted to comply, while Mam sat downstairs wearing one of her two remaining expressions. Neither parent had ever offered much in the way of support, but the girls knew that any assistance that had come their way in the past would come no more.

What with payments now due to the doctor, gravedigger and carpenter, the death of the boys dealt the family a near-fatal financial blow. Any money saved from years of hard work, Pa used to maintain an unflagging state of drunkenness. Lou busied herself in the kitchen, calculating stocks of flour, apples and potatoes against the remaining eight family members and the remaining months of winter. The result offered no encouragement, and her busy preparation of meals disguised a rising anxiety. Slicing vegetables into a deep iron kettle with a precious bit of lard, she added dried sage and thyme from the summer garden, and cooked the mixture slowly over the fire, attempting to invoke the spirit of stew. But even having performed all of her considerable magic, the meals remained stubbornly short of satisfying.

They ate in silence, Sally fussing for more bread where there was none, Mam translucent with sorrow, Pa snoring drunkenly beside his soup and Lou pressing a portion of her meagre share on to Ellen, who sat beside her, staring wretchedly at her plate. Pell took as many meals as was seemly at Finches'. And all of this Bean observed with his silent all-noticing eyes.

What he decided he told no one, with the exception of Pell, eventually, by his actions in the dark, on the morning she awoke with a blind determination to leave home.

23

Robert Ames took Pell to meet a woman as sour-faced as his mother, who looked her over as if she were a market pig and led her up a narrow staircase in the stone barn to a tiny dark room that stank of old milk. In it lay a straw mattress without even a cover or blanket, and nothing else.

'You'll be needing to keep it decent,' she said, scowling at Pell. 'No visitors, no drink, and I'll not be having that thieving dog round here neither.'

Pell tried to imagine what visitors she might consider inviting round to the stinking tomb, while the woman kept talking on the subject of sin, and 'every girl's sworn duty to avoid foul temptations'. She pronounced the words with poisonous disdain as if they had the power to corrupt the very tongue that spoke them.

Pell left Dicken chained up with Robert at the forge, where he pined until the moment she escaped from the dairy and came to him. Each evening she held his head in her hands and ran her aching fingers through the thick ruff of fur round his neck, full of remorse at his imprisonment. And despite his impatience for food and freedom he burrowed against her, sighing devotion until she set him free.

It pained her to keep him tied up day and night but it was

impossible to do otherwise. Work commenced before first light and lasted until after dark, and sixty cows required leading from pasture to dairy yard to be milked, and back again, twice a day. In addition, there was the churning, the lifting, turning and wetting of cheeses, the hauling of buckets so heavy they left Pell's fingers ridged and bloody, the cleaning and mucking out, and a thousand other duties. Robert's aunt, Osborne (after her dead husband, no 'Mrs' Osborne either), seemed determined to wring as much value as possible from the daily shilling she paid her workers, minus sixpence a week for lodging. Instead of six milkers for her sixty cows, she employed only four, and girls, being cheaper. Supervising all of the work herself saved additionally on a foreman. Local people told of the water she added to her milk and the chalk to her cheese, forcing her to find markets further abroad; and as to the health and vitality of her employees she was perfectly indifferent.

On Pell's first day of employment, Osborne cornered her in the cool room and pinned her with a narrow dead gaze. 'I don't know what a girl like you is doing in this place, but my nephew's due to marry four weeks hence.' She paused to let this fact sink in, and not satisfied with Pell's reaction added, 'And a nice decent girl she is too.'

'In which case, I wish him every happiness,' replied Pell stiffly.

'Do not pretend you misunderstand my meaning,' hissed the older woman.

Pell said nothing. No words would alter the fact of Osborne's dislike. When the woman turned on her heel and departed, Pell trembled with unexpressed feeling. She would not acknowledge her humiliation.

In her meanness, Osborne offered nothing but bread for the

evening meal, and Pell learned to scrounge and save slivers of cheese when she could. The discarded rinds she saved for Dicken, who gnawed them happily. Even in the poorest town, enough was thrown away to keep a dog fed.

When she could, Pell sat with Robert Ames at the forge for her supper. Robert teased her about the stink of old milk and cheese in her clothing and hair, but she barely smelled it any more. Sometimes she watched him work, silently correcting him where she knew she might do better. He merely grinned when she told him she'd learned the farrier's trade in Nomansland, so unable was he to imagine any female at such work.

One evening, a pale-haired girl with tidy features and a pretty, peevish mouth interrupted them, and Robert introduced her as his wife-to-be, Cecily. Pell smiled when Robert took the girl's hand in his, but the girl did not smile back, and Pell wondered at the number of enemies she had made merely by virtue of an acquaintance with Robert Ames.

Osborne's own daughters had long since given up the backbreaking hours of dairy work in favour of marriage to farmers, one with a little shop outside Salisbury, the other nearer to home. The sisters had hoped to be set up as milliners by their doting father, to sell lengths of silk ribbons and finely plaited crowns. But he had died of overwork inconveniently young, and the dream of the hat shop dissolved. What neither girl would consider was the sort of work Pell did, the dawn-to-dusk slavery for their embittered mother. They were a close family, Osborne assured Pell, but neither daughter came to visit.

Pell stayed three weeks in Pevesy. She bit her tongue and worked the long, exhausting hours, but Osborne's mean ways made each day a trial. Her acquaintance with Robert Ames flourished in the face of so much opposition, but Pell would not be alone with him, nor even call him her friend, for propriety's sake. And yet his family and his bride-to-be buzzed around her like wasps.

One evening at dusk, as Pell returned from a visit to the forge, Robert Ames's fiancée appeared at her side, silent as a vole, with a face like stone. She pinched Pell's arm hard and stared at her, lips pursed, eyes drawn together in a squint of fury. 'If I tell you where to find the man you seek, will you leave us for good?'

Pell nodded, stifling the impulse to cry out.

'My father bought a rabbiting dog from a man, a poacher they say, a few miles out of town.' She held out a slip of paper with a map sketched on it, but as Pell reached to take it the other girl snatched it back. 'Only if you promise to leave and not come back here. *Ever.*'

Again Pell nodded, and Cecily slapped the paper into her hand. 'Take it and be damned,' hissed the girl in her pretty little voice, and hurried away.

The next day, having collected her few belongings and her last week's salary, Pell fetched Dicken and walked out on to the road, thinking of nothing but the future. She did not say goodbye to Robert Ames or to his aunt.

24

The sketch was not easy to follow, and Pell wondered if she'd been lured away on a hoax. No distances were marked, and only a scrawled reference to an inn indicated that she might be on the right road. They made slow progress, doubling back at every wrong turn and false trail, and sometimes standing where two paths crossed, unable to choose forward, backward, left or right as a direction.

Darkness descended rapidly and it began to rain. A general feeling of wretchedness overtook her, and with no obvious shelter nearby, she and Dicken crawled into the base of a large dead tree that offered some small protection from the wind. A colder, more lonely place could barely exist on earth, Pell thought, and though she was not much given to tears, she cried and cried, her entire body shaking with desolation. Dicken licked at the tears for salt and when she pushed him away, lay quietly, waiting for her to be once more what she was.

They curled together in the night like wild things.

The next morning, aching and chilled to the bone, she turned off along a road so narrow and overgrown that she felt certain they'd gone wrong, or that the girl had played a trick on her. She studied the sketchy lines on the paper, turning it round and round, and even when most convinced she was lost for good, couldn't bring herself to consider another plan.

The sky was a rough grey sea, splashing great plumes of rain through the wood, and Pell ducked her head low against wet branches that crisscrossed their path. Increasingly it looked as if the last person to travel this way had done so months or even years before.

At a turn in the path, a fallen tree blocked the way and she stopped. Dicken waited patiently while she stood listening to the creaking wood. It groaned and chattered to her in its strange familiar language, and eventually, with a sigh, Pell began to push through the dense undergrowth as best she could, limping around the far edge of the great vertical spread of roots. Brambles and nettles tore at her clothing, but Dicken tiptoed behind her weight-lessly, placing each foot with precision before choosing a spot for the next. She emerged at last on to the path, brushed herself down, and walked only another hundred paces before the wood opened abruptly on to a long sloping meadow, washed clean by the rain and lit by a break in the sullen sky. Even Dicken stopped to look.

As Pell stared, Dicken bolted suddenly into the tall autumn grass. A moment later he sprang up, locked in growling embrace with a large paper-thin dog, whom the golden field rendered nearly invisible. The strange dog bowled and pinned him in no time, holding him with a firm grip on the throat that tightened when Dicken tried to wriggle free.

'Leave him!' Pell shouted, trying to get a grip on the assailant, who slipped through her fingers like flax. Flipping and struggling on the ground, the dogs formed a single tangle of snarling fur, till all at once the strange dog released his grip and raced off. Dicken shot back to Pell like the youngster he still was, and pressed himself against her, trembling with nervous elation and fear.

Pell followed the other dog's progress through the grass, and at last caught sight of the man. He had the sun behind him, but his outline was unmistakeable. He stopped when he saw her, and they stared at each other, one no less surprised than the other. She strode towards him.

'I want my brother,' she said, 'and my horse.'

His expression was blank.

'*And* my money.'

'What has any of this to do with me?'

'Your friend Harris is a thief.'

She saw him pause for the briefest instant. 'Whatever he's done is not my affair.'

'*Whose* affair, then?' The colour in her cheeks rose and her eyes glinted with fury. 'Look at the state of me! He left me with *nothing.*'

They glared at each other for a long moment until his dogs settled the matter. Spying a hare across the meadow, they raced from his side in pursuit with Dicken close behind. The hare led the chase in long muscular bounds, swerving left and right, flipping backwards along her length, and for a long moment it looked as if she was not to be caught. But the dogs stuck to her without wavering, one swapping the lead with the other, not losing position even when she changed direction, until finally it seemed as if the dauntless creature was finished. They hadn't accounted for Dicken, however. Half a second's enthusiastic distraction was all it took and the hare was gone, through a thicket of thorns where the dogs could only race back and forth, whining frustration. Pell silently applauded the hare.

Dogman looked at her. 'I haven't got your money and I know nothing of the horse. Or the child. I'll have a word with Harris next I see him.'

Pell stared, her face flushed with anger. 'A *word*? And how is that to help? Harris is a thief and *you* let him cheat me.'

He sighed. 'I'm hardly responsible for every horse trader in Salisbury. It could be months before our paths cross again. And as for the horse, he'll be long gone. It's Harris's business, trading horses. He doesn't keep them to admire.'

'What about my brother?'

Dogman frowned. 'I can't see what Harris would be wanting with a child.'

Defeat silenced her. It was not at all impossible that Bean had followed Harris of his own free will. Her shoulders sagged. 'When will you see him?'

'Could be five, six months.'

She gasped. '*Impossible.*'

He shrugged and walked off.

'Come back!' Grabbing his sleeve, she pulled him round to face her. 'How do you expect me to live?'

'That's your affair.' His eyes were cold.

'You *owe* me.'

'I owe you nothing.'

She followed him as he strode off along a path even narrower than the one she'd been travelling. The dense growth scraped past her, leaving raw tracks across her arms and face. Ahead of her, Dogman never slowed his pace, nor turned to look.

She emerged behind him in a clearing before a worn stone cottage. Pell could just see the edge of a kitchen garden along the south side of the house. In a well-built enclosure just beyond, a spotted sow basked in the sunshine and, behind, two rows of shabby kennels stood side by side.

Dogman opened the door, then turned to face the defiant girl and her dog.

'Well?'

Tears sprang unbidden to her eyes. 'I'm not leaving.'

'Suit yourself,' he said, 'I'm no conjurer.'

'I'll wait. There is nothing else for me to do.'

Exasperation got the better of him. '*Where* will you wait?'

She cast about – at the house, the makeshift kennels, the hen-house, woodshed and finally, some distance away, a half-ruined brick building that might once have housed cows. Instead of answering, she stepped across to it, finding it neglected and empty. It smelled of animals, but looked dry enough.

This will have to do, she thought. Despite having no hearth or proper windows, there was straw for a bed, and plenty more could be gathered, and if she could live under cover and within four walls for the winter she would make do and not freeze. When Dogman produced her money or a better idea occurred to her, she would move on. But not till then.

When she turned round to gauge his reaction, he had gone.

25

Pell and Dogman lived side by side without giving away that either knew the other existed.

She took water from his well and walked twice a week to the nearest village, four miles away, for bread. She took Dicken out to catch rabbits that she gutted and skinned and sold in town, and even made two acquaintances, Miss Eliza Leape and her brother William, owners of the village bakery. Miss Leape greeted the ragged duo with more enthusiasm than Pell had met in some time.

'So, you are the girl who lives with the poacher!'

'I do not live with him,' Pell replied, surprised and discomfited.

'I've glimpsed him once or twice,' the woman confided. 'He is very handsome, though not at all refined.'

Pell said nothing, only looked away.

Eliza gazed past Pell into some hazy middle distance, stoking her own romantic dreams. 'Has he . . .' Here she paused, assuming an air of delicacy. 'Has he . . . made advances?'

Repelled by this line of questioning, Pell turned to go.

'Oh, please stay,' begged the girl, but the instant Pell relented she began again. 'Are you very much in love with him?'

Pell flushed with outrage. 'Why do you speak to me this way?'

The girl's eyes widened rapturously and she clapped her hands. 'I can tell by your face that you are! And have you encouraged him?' Eliza's voice turned sly. 'I would. Though of course I would never let it be known that we –'

'There is nothing between us,' Pell said coldly.

'Of course there isn't,' replied Eliza with a wink. 'But do take pity on me! I've been bursting with curiosity to meet the mysterious beauty who lives in the wood.'

It was impossible to recognize this description of herself, and Pell made her escape. Her relief at leaving the village was so great that she nearly ran the miles back to her home in the little barn. Thereafter, temptation to avoid the baker and her brother was strong, but she scolded herself for it. Perhaps this journey has made me strange, she thought, for I never noticed before how very little I like ordinary human society.

Dogman set out hunting each day at dusk, and only if she happened to see him in the early dawn, and then only by the weight of the bag on his shoulder, could she tell what he'd caught. Birds were light, rabbits heavier. Sometimes there would be two or three big hares strung up across his back. Most days he returned in the dark while she still slept, and they might go two or three days without laying eyes on each other, or exchanging even the most cursory nod.

She did not like him. He had no humanity about him, and an abrupt way of closing down even the briefest exchange. His nature was cold and unyielding, and the only evidence she had of human warmth was the dialogue he carried on with his animals.

If I were a hound, she thought, or a ferret, or even a rat, he would show more interest in my troubles than he does now.

The two of them shared nothing willingly – not conversation, meals, or information from town. But Dicken had other plans. Within a week, he could be found scrambling for the carcasses and entrails that were tossed into the kennels each morning and, despite Pell's fury at his willingness to befriend her enemy, in some obscure way she was grateful for it too.

She noted, too, that Dogman didn't chase him away.

And then one evening, Dicken disappeared. She feared that he'd come off badly in a fight with a stoat or a fox and lay injured and bleeding somewhere, but no matter how long and how loudly she called, he did not appear. Having searched the kennels and the outbuildings, she walked for hours on narrow lanes and paths, covering miles in the dark, shouting his name and whistling, falling over branches and into ditches and jumping at every noise and shadow.

She returned exhausted to the barn and slept fitfully, until the hour before dawn and the end of a poacher's day, when he gambolled home, greeting her with all the enthusiasm of a long-lost friend, and not a whit of conscience. His coat was muddy and thick with burrs and seeds, and he had a bad bite on one side of his face caked black with blood, but he trembled with happiness and Pell could almost fancy he grinned at her. She cleaned his wounds as best she could, and tied him indoors, cursing Dogman. But Dicken paced and whined and sulked until she let him go, and then he was off to the kennels like a shot, hanging back while the other dogs ate their fill, and then darting in for leftovers as befitted his lowly status.

Later that morning, she nearly tripped over a plucked and cleaned pheasant on her doorstep. Dogman was nowhere to be seen.

She intercepted him at dusk as he set off with his dogs.

'What is this?' she asked, holding up the bird.

'Looks like a pheasant.'

'Stolen?'

He shrugged. 'Likely to be.'

'Am I to be jailed for thievery?'

He almost smiled. 'Only if you turn yourself over to the law. Don't forget to take your dog. He killed it.'

'You've made a criminal of him, then.' She knew she sounded absurd.

Dogman raised an eyebrow. 'He comes by it naturally. Leave it at my door if you don't want it.'

She cooked the pheasant that night over an open fire. On his return from hunting, Dicken crunched through the carcass.

Another week passed. It had become bitter cold in the cowshed. In desperation, she lit a fire in one corner; it produced a roomful of smoke but no warmth. Piling stones into a rough hearth against an outer wall, Pell kept the fire fed day and night with wood she collected herself. She might have helped herself to Dogman's woodpile while he was out, but would not lower herself to steal. Or to ask. The fire heated the wall, until the bricks absorbed enough to warm her at night. It wasn't much, but better than none. A thick layer of straw, hay and grass protected her from the freezing ground and she piled more hay between her blankets and on top of her to sleep. She desperately missed Dicken's warmth.

With one living in darkness and the other in daylight, Pell and Dogman barely glimpsed each other. But Dicken loped more and more between the two, first leaning towards and then adopting the realm of the night, so that now he returned to her only at dawn. Then he would sleep, so that he became useless to her, despite the spoils she found by her door most mornings. She counted Dicken's days as a hunter by his wounds, until she lost count. There were gouges and tears, more often than not a limp, or dried blood that, once cleaned, gave way to puncture marks where he'd been bitten – whether by his quarry or one of his companions was impossible to tell. These wounds she dressed, and as soon as the next night's hunting came round, he cried and paced, desperate to go out again.

Pell had been living in the cowshed for nearly a month when Dicken returned home with a particularly nasty bite on his hind leg. Despite her attentions it refused to heal and she watched, helpless, as it began to ooze a foul-smelling pus, causing him to hobble about on three legs and whimper in his sleep. She tied him indoors and walked to town for herbal medicines, using her precious store of shillings for powders and poultices that did not work, and bandages that Dicken tore off and left in tatters. As she ran out of options, she became increasingly frightened, and on the day she awoke to find him shivering and dull-eyed with pain, she hammered on Dogman's door.

He opened it at last, half asleep, pulling on a shirt with the hand that wasn't holding a shotgun, and she stared at him for a long moment, unable to ask for help.

'My dog,' she said at last. 'He's ill. I've tried what I know . . .'

He followed her to the cowshed and knelt beside the animal, lifting the poultice she had wrapped round his leg. They both caught the stink of rotting flesh.

He looked at the wound, prodded it with his finger, then replaced the bandage and left. A surge of wrath rose up in her. It was *his fault* they were here, *his fault* she had no money, *his fault* her dog lay dying. And him so uncaring that all he could manage was to walk away and leave her to cope alone with the situation *he* had wrought. She held her head in her hands, shaking with fear and rage, and cold.

But he was back, with a twist of paper and instructions for Pell to hold Dicken while he placed one hand over the dog's muzzle, parted the lips of the wound and poured a vivid yellow powder straight into the suppurating flesh. The dog struggled wildly, but Pell kept one hand firmly against his flank, and the other on his shoulder, while Dogman talked to him in the low voice Pell remembered from the fair. After a few attempts to struggle free, Dicken dropped back, exhausted.

Dogman stroked his head and stood up. 'Have him take water if he will.' And then, without looking at Pell, he went out.

Pell sat with her dog, thinking of every animal she'd ever nursed, the ones she'd saved and the others. She tried to dribble water down his throat, but his head lolled sideways, so watery saliva spooled out on to the dirt floor. His eyes looked sunken and he panted in harsh, ugly rasps that sucked his ribcage nearly flat. He no longer seemed to recognize her voice.

At twilight she left him, to fetch water from the well and escape the sound of his breathing. When she returned some time later, he lifted his head a little in greeting. Later that night he managed to swallow when she dribbled water into his mouth, and feebly tried to lap more. She let him drink until his head rolled back and his eyes closed, then ran to the kennels to find Dogman and give him the news. He didn't change expression, only tapped his pipe against one leg and nodded, and when she thanked him he turned his back on her and appeared not to have heard.

Pell kept Dicken away from the kennels for more than a week, until he had lost his limp and the wound began to turn pale and flat. She and Dogman encountered one another more frequently, whether by chance or design was impossible to know. She was less careful to avoid him, but he was no more cordial than before. He continued to treat his animals with more courtesy than he treated her, acknowledging her not at all.

By this time, Pell and the baker's girl had become familiar enough to exchange histories, for surely it was the responsibility of itinerant buyers of bread to provide not only rabbits and pheasants in exchange, but stories as well. Pell's story of leaving Nomansland greatly pleased Eliza, who had seen her sister married off to a man in greater need of a servant, she said, than a wife. She had watched her sister grow ill with overwork, and finally die of a fever caught after the birth of her third daughter. At the funeral, the husband had turned the children over to Eliza and refused to have them back, saying he had no use for girls. The three children were all that remained of her sister's short life, and for Eliza and her brother, surrogate parents to the unwanted babes, they served as lasting, hungry reminders of only one of the ways a marriage might end.

Eliza told this story with mournful satisfaction, and swore to Pell that she would never marry. Her vow inspired sympathy from Pell, who chose not to notice how well such a position suited the girl's plain face and advanced years.

In exchange, Pell gradually revealed her reasons for leaving home, and much of what had happened since, and Eliza listened to what she called Pell's 'adventures' with the rapt attention of a woman who has never strayed more than a mile or two from her place of birth. When it came to the reality of Pell's life in the woods, however, Eliza had no interest, and clung to her own version of the story.

There was, of course, no flirtation with Dogman to pass the hours the way Eliza insisted upon imagining it, and the freezing shed was not nearly so adorable and snug as she painted it. Pell's days were spent covered in rabbit blood and gore, collecting wood and plucking birds, fetching heavy buckets of water from the well, and worrying about the months to come. The dairy money was nearly gone and when winter rabbits became scarce she would have nothing left to barter. Her grey woollen dress had been patched so many times that the apron she wore could no longer be depended upon to conceal the holes. She saved her stockings by walking barefoot except on the very worst days, and meanwhile grudged the farthing's worth of wool it took to mend them. It grew colder day by day, and how she would cope when the ground froze hard, she had no idea.

She voiced these doubts to her friend, and Eliza's eyes widened. 'Can you knead bread and shape loaves?' she asked.

Pell nodded. Despite her preference for outdoor pursuits, she could bake as well as any girl brought up in a village too small for its own bakery.

'Well, come here and assist us! William and I are always in need of help, and we'll pay you in bread when money's short. You might even stay here with us if you can be parted from your poacher. We'd have a lovely time, like sisters!'

Pell accepted the offer with gratitude. She dreaded the relentless hardship of winter and imagined a room with a fire and perhaps even hot water to wash. Despite her misgivings about Eliza, the possibility of paid work refuelled her optimism. She suspected that her habit of conversing with Dicken was making her odder and less fit for human society with each passing day. The few villagers who greeted her did so warily, for a girl of her age and uncertain provenance living in some unclear arrangement with the local poacher did not comply with anyone's idea of respectability.

There were even some who imagined – with a thrill of outrage – that Pell might attempt to attend the village church, and steps were taken to cope with so heinous a situation, should it arise. Such were the amusements of village life.

26

Eliza's brother William, older by four or five years, shared with his sister a wide open face in which there was nothing of malice, though in his case, not much of wit either. According to their father's last will and testament, the bakery belonged to the son, but for the past seven years it had been Eliza who worked long hours kneading bread, keeping the accounts, negotiating at market for the sacks of grain necessary to their trade, and supervising the shop, on top of cleaning, cooking, sewing and caring for the three orphaned girls. William's contributions were more abstract. He provided a 'manly presence', as he described it (to prevent his sister being cheated by dishonest vendors), stood at the front of the shop smiling broadly at the customers, and relit the ovens when the overworked Eliza allowed them to go cold. Although the little girls would soon be old enough to help, William felt the time had come to acquire a son and heir. And thus, a wife.

He might have had more luck with village girls had there been more of them, but an epidemic of fever in his youth had led to a shortfall, which made Pell's mysterious arrival in the village all the more providential. No other family could have considered Pell an acceptable match, but between Eliza and William there was no parent to object, and together they felt that they would be doing the girl a great favour by agreeing to overlook her many disadvantages of birth and situation.

William's decision to propose marriage caused Eliza great delight; the fact that Pell showed no signs of being similarly inclined discouraged neither of them.

And so, the die was cast.

A number of little social engagements followed, each couched in the most innocent of terms. A supper, attended by all three, was a pleasant affair. A little tea party, presided over by Eliza, was considered perfectly successful, despite the fact that every guest but Pell declined to attend.

'Could you come to town on Friday,' Eliza asked, a few days later, 'and help in the shop? Christmas is coming and we have far more work than we two can manage.'

Pell was glad to oblige, glad for the pay and the occupation. That Eliza was missing when she arrived did not surprise her in the least, for the little girls were often ailing, or the accounts required updating, or the house needed sweeping. Pell and William worked quietly side by side for most of the morning, with Dicken asleep nearby. Pell took on the lion's share of mixing and measuring, shaping the yeasty dough into squares and oblongs, and carefully timing them in the big brick oven. She noticed that William seemed preoccupied, on several occasions standing for long minutes in the centre of the room clasping and unclasping his hands and moving his lips silently. He worked uncomfortably close to her and, though she was invariably polite, she thought how much she'd rather share these chores with Eliza than her strange, awkward brother.

Eliza appeared once or twice, pulling her brother aside for some consultation or other, which Pell ignored. Until at the very last, he turned to her trembling, with trickles of sweat carving trails in the floury surface of his face.

'What is it, William?' Pell moved towards him with concern. 'Are you unwell?'

For an answer, he dropped to his knees and buried his head in her skirts, his powerful arms wrapped vice-like round her thighs. 'I love you, Miss Ridley,' came the muffled voice, as she struggled to free herself, 'and I wish above all things to make you my wife.'

The horror of the scene came over her slowly. So unexpected was his declaration that her first reaction was disbelief. 'Please stand up, William. Please. You . . . you are very kind, and I am flattered by your offer, but surely you must see that I cannot possibly marry you.'

He did not loosen his grip. 'You must. I wish it above all things.'

'Let me go, William, please.' She saw the colour begin to rise in his face and felt the first stirrings of unease. 'William? William, I beg you . . . let me go.' The first time she said his name, it was with all the civility she could muster, but when he not only failed to release her, but pressed his head more firmly against her skirts, she began to push against his shoulders and then to shout, pounding his back with her fists. 'Let me go! William, for pity's sake! What would Eliza think?' If only her friend would return and put a stop to the awful scene. But if Eliza could hear, she made no move to help.

'Give me the answer I require!' moaned William, nuzzling deep between her thighs, his huge hands grasping and clutching at her.

Pell struggled with all her strength. 'Let me go!' she cried, and finally, simply, '*Stop!*'

This word appeared at last to penetrate the deep haze of his passion. He dropped his arms to his sides, hanging his head like a great ruined beast as she staggered backwards. For an instant she watched in horror, certain he would begin to sob, and her brain swam with panic and doubt. Had she inspired the misunderstanding? Had she somehow led him to believe she felt something for him? Nothing could have been further from the truth. She reached out and placed one hand on his shoulder. 'I'm sorry, William, I would not knowingly hurt you –'

He raised his head, unable to see anything but the carefully constructed plans for his future in ruins. Roaring his pain like a wounded bull, he clambered to his feet and clamped a huge hand on her arm. 'You would not hurt me? Would not *hurt me*?' He seemed blind, now, with humiliation and fury. And then he hit her hard across the face, the force of the blow hurling her across the room, smashing her head against the hot iron of the oven door. She tried to catch herself, but twisted round on one arm as she fell. He followed, lifting her up once more as she struggled against him, crying and shouting for help. Grasping her by the hair, he trapped her against the wall, pushed her head back and shoved his mouth on top of hers, pressing his great flaccid tongue between her lips and forcing himself hard against her.

'William!' Eliza flew across to him and he let Pell drop, staggering back with a moan of pain as if he, not she, were the injured party.

'Thank God,' murmured Pell. 'Thank God you've arrived . . .'

Eliza looked at her, and her features expressed not sympathy but anger. 'What did you say to him? What did you say to provoke him?'

Pell balanced carefully on both feet, swaying with pain, her burnt face already beginning to swell. The blood streamed down from a gash over one eye, her left arm cradled her right. She faced Eliza with dignity. 'I said I would not marry him. Would you expect me to be convinced otherwise by his argument?'

Cheeks flaming, Eliza turned away. 'How else did you expect him to react? He was terribly disappointed, weren't you, my poor William?'

William stood panting and close to tears. He nodded, dumbly, like a child.

'Won't you reconsider, Pell?' Eliza's voice had turned dripping and golden, like syrup. 'It was only the sincerity of his passion that carried him away, wasn't it, Will? He'll make a wonderful husband . . .'

As Pell moved towards the door, Eliza went to her brother, embracing him and tenderly wiping the tears from his eyes as she kissed him over and over on his face and lips. 'Don't cry, dear William, don't cry. Pell *will* marry you after all, of course she will, won't you, dear? Don't cry, dearest. There, there.'

27

Pell stumbled the miles of narrow roads to her home, leaning on Dicken with the arm that didn't cause pain, and drank deeply from the bucket by the well when she arrived. She collapsed on to her straw bed and lay motionless throughout the night and all of the next day, despite Dicken's insistence that she rise and greet him. She felt no hunger, only a vast thirst and an ever-increasing pain in her arm, but if she ignored both she found she could stand it, or that the pain disappeared for hours at a time as she drifted in and out of wakefulness. She wanted only to shut her eyes against the world forever.

Two days had passed when she heard Dicken greet Dogman at the door with a whine of pleasure. He said her name and when she didn't answer, went away again.

When he returned the following day and again received no answer, he entered the little cowshed and found her feverish and damp, her face swollen black and green, one arm laid beside her at an unnatural angle. He said not a word, but gathered her up in his arms, a little shocked at how easily this was accomplished, and took her to his cottage, making a bed for her by the fire.

He gave her brandy to drink until her eyes rolled back and closed, and then he felt the broken arm through the swelling and pulled it back into position while she lay still, her face twisted in pain. He set the arm in strips of cloth dipped in egg white, exactly as he had set a multitude of broken animal limbs, relieved that the bone had not pierced the skin. The burns on her face he cleaned with a cloth soaked in boiled water, and for the fever he administered liquorice and henbane tea. Her injuries were no worse than those he treated daily in his kennels; the mortal injury of a dog was something to which he had grown accustomed but not resigned.

He left her each night to go out, and on the fourth day he returned with his dogs in the morning to find her quiet, no longer tossing and babbling in waking sleep. She opened her eyes, seemed to recognize him at last and for an instant glared at him and croaked out, 'Where is . . . my money . . .?' Her eyes drooped and fell shut before she could see that for the first time in many days he had smiled.

When she awoke the following morning, Pell at first thought she was back home in Nomansland, in her old bed with Lou. For a time she lay still, waiting for the shriek of squabbling siblings, for the sound of the tin tea caddy being opened, and the china clink as the top of the teapot was replaced. She even blinked sleepily, and tried to sit up before realizing that one arm was bound up in a splint, and one eye still swollen nearly shut. Her face hurt.

When Dogman returned from hunting, she attempted to deliver a speech, telling him that she appreciated all he'd done (what precisely *had* he done?) and would now be going. But he told her not to speak, and went as usual to prepare food for himself and the dogs, leaving her to sleep again, and to wonder, as she fell asleep, what would happen next.

He gave her broth that was cloudy and strong tasting, and with her one good arm she lifted it to her lips and drank it herself. Her limbs were bruised and tender, and one side of her face didn't seem to belong to her. She remembered what had happened but couldn't think how she had arrived here. The effort of remembering tired her, and she drifted off to sleep.

When next he returned, she felt so much better that she sat up and declared herself well enough to leave. If he would help her to gather herself, she would cease to impose upon his kindness. She was most apologetic for inconveniencing him as long as she had.

He said nothing but waited; watched her swing her feet on to the floor and then sit trembling, until she dropped back on the bed once more.

He did not lift a hand to help.

When she opened her eyes sometime later, they met his, dark and serious. He felt the broken arm carefully and set it down again, apparently satisfied with her progress. And left her, to see to his dogs.

The time came to replace the bandage with a fresh one, and the following day he unwrapped it quickly, holding the arm so she could see for herself the violent multicoloured bruising. He wrapped it again in clean strips of cloth, binding it more tightly this time. She made not a sound while he worked, but watched him, the pain causing his face to swim before her eyes.

Two more days passed, and at last she was strong enough to sit without help. Dogman crossed the room to her with beef tea, but when he held her eyes and observed that she neither flinched nor looked away, he sat beside her on the bed, placed the tea on the floor, took her face in his hands and kissed her, with consideration for her injuries but without shame or caution. And when he had done kissing her, he returned to the big room with its wood stove and open fire to cook his breakfast.

28

From that day on they lived as man and wife, though no mention was made of the change. He still went out poaching each night, and brought game back to sell, or to salt and preserve for the winter, coming to her in the hours before sunrise smelling of blood and earth. She accepted the permission bestowed by passion to live entirely in the present.

In the solitary stone house with its roaring fire and orderly stores of food, Pell experienced waves of feeling she could barely acknowledge. But she found safety too. While he slept, exhausted from a night's work, she lay awake beside him, wondering how she happened to be here.

'Are you asleep?' Her mind could not rest in daylight.

'Yes.' Eyes closed, he pulled her close.

'Listen to the wind. We shall need more wood in.'

He would not be roused.

'There'll be no hunting tonight.'

'Hush.'

And a little while later, 'The dogs are dreaming.' By the fire she could hear the high-pitched yips of their somnolent chase.

He half opened an eye, and yawned. 'Of what?'

'Of rabbits.' It was daylight but howling a storm. She could see her breath, and the fire needed stoking. Yet she could not bring herself to leave. 'I've things to do.'

'Yes, go,' he murmured, adjusting the grip of his arms so that she could not. When eventually she pulled free, he slept on, undisturbed.

She told him about Birdie and Bean and how she happened to be out in the world alone, but learned nothing about his past. She also told how she'd come to be injured, and as he listened his eyes narrowed.

The following week he returned from hunting with a package wrapped in brown paper. She unwrapped it slowly. Within, lay a hunting knife, small and razor sharp, in a slim leather sheath. She looked at him.

'For next time,' he said, and showed her how to slide the knife in its sheath into the top of her boot each morning, until after a time it became a habit so ordinary, she nearly forgot its existence.

His two coursing dogs lived in the house, and he allowed Dicken to stay as well, for the dog wouldn't leave her, and wailed for hours if locked in the kennels with his terriers.

He was, she learned, a hunter by trade and a poacher by choice. His father and grandfather and great-grandfather had been gamekeepers since before the enclosures, but the niceties of employment did not suit him.

We are both outcasts, she thought.

She did not want to live idly and, once recovered, she swapped two big hares for two laying hens, then the following week two more, until she had six hens, which would mean forty-two eggs a week when the warm weather came.

On some days, the butcher's cart came along the road. The

butcher would buy whatever Dogman had killed and save her a trip to the market at St Mary's. With the proceeds, she bought flour and tea, as there was no shortage of game. She tended the parsnips, leeks and potatoes in Dogman's garden, piling manure and straw around the plants to keep them safe from winter frosts. He never asked her to cook for him but she did, and when they ate together, her day was ending and his just beginning. He cleaned his gun and traps while she fed the hens and knitted new stockings with wool she bought in town. Before the hard days of winter set in, he slaughtered the pig, and for a week stayed at home with the job of butchering. The dogs feasted on bones and scraps and Pell roasted the head. Dogman salted the flitches and sold the rest.

When he returned to hunting, her own company and the company of the hens suited her perfectly. Dicken showed up one morning, proudly holding one of her best layers limp and terrified in his mouth, and she scolded him, returned the distressed creature to the hen house and constructed a makeshift lock for the door out of leather pulled through two holes and knotted tightly. Dogman raised an eyebrow at the inelegant contraption, but it kept predators out. Dicken only dared stalk the hens if she were absent. She had seen him from the window on sunny days, sliding close on his belly and staring at them hungrily when they picked and pecked at the earth. Sometimes she felt sorry for him, his instincts so at odds with hers.

On occasion, she allowed for the possibility that her condition resembled love. She was busy, had enough to eat and enough solitude and, in addition, something like a deep attachment to another person. His passion seemed to release her from a long confinement and she felt free for the first time since her days racing Jack across the heath. And yet, while Bean's disappearance remained unsolved, she could not be happy.

Sometimes she imagined him dead – murdered or starved or drowned, unable to cry out, with no one to save him or give him a decent burial. She saw him exploited and left to rot because he had no voice to protest or say who he was.

As much as she might try to shut him out of her brain, she could not. By not searching she continued to fail him.

Towards this end, she went on foot through all the parishes she could reach in a day's travel from Pevesy, asking at each if a boy matching Bean's description had been found. She visited every workhouse, finding exactly the same in each – squalor, hunger, misery, disease. At each place, she was told the same: 'No one of that description has been brought here.' But she searched every corner regardless, saw the silent babies with robin-bright eyes, swaddled tight and left to stare at the ceiling in tidy rows; the elderly, or the prematurely aged, packed four or six to a bed, their rheumatic bones clacking, their withered limbs shifting, vainly, in search of comfort or warmth; the crippled and the mentally incompetent, lumped together to torment each other day and night. Worst of all were the able bodied, the unfortunate or unlucky, who had somehow slipped over the line that separated respectability from penury and collapse. These were women abandoned by men, the ill or injured, widows or widowers, and children – unwanted, orphaned or deficient in some way. She left each place, alone, with equal measures of relief and despair.

At every village she asked for information. But Bean, it seemed, had melted away as surely as water into sand. Her journeys accomplished nothing, except to remind her how large was the area she searched, and how small the child she sought.

29

Pell depended increasingly on Dogman's poaching, and on selling what he caught. The butcher in town never asked where her hares came from, and it was best for all that he didn't. She had heard of poachers being gaoled, or shot on sight, or hanged, and yet no village butcher went so far as to imagine life without wild meat, come by honestly, or by other means.

When game was scarce, he limed birds, selling robins and finches to dealers from London, who profited from the fashion for keeping a songbird or two in a cage by the front door. Birds of prey he sold to gypsies. Deer were rarely taken due to their size and the danger of being caught, but fox pelts fetched a good price for coats and collars. Stolen pheasants had to be sold far from the manor on which they'd been bred, but were otherwise profitable, and even the thin winter rabbits earned something.

Pell helped to repair his bird nets and oil the hinges on his traps; he showed her how to render the sticky lime from holly sap and mutton fat, and afterwards to clean glue from the bird's feathers in readiness for sale. She learned to prepare skins (fox, weasel, even badger) that sold for anything from a few shillings to a few pounds, depending on condition and supply.

He was twice her age, and she wondered at his past.

One early evening as he dressed to go out with his dogs, she remained in bed watching him.

'Have you always lived like this?'

'Like this?'

'Alone.'

He raised an eyebrow. 'Would you call me alone?'

'Alone, but for me.'

'I see,' he said, pulling on one boot, then the other. And then after a minute, soberly, 'No, not always.'

'Ah.'

'I once lived with a hunter named Plummer.'

She waited, but he volunteered no more and at last she sighed. 'You are full of secrets.'

'It is women who love secrets.'

'What secrets have I? A birthplace; parents; siblings – dead, alive and lost; an almost-husband, abandoned; a horse, gone. A man who owes me money. There is nothing mysterious in *me*. But you! You have no past, and nobody but yourself.'

'Nobody apart from dogs, badgers, foxes and a horde of gamekeepers at my heels.' He looked up, amused. 'And you. A multitude, I would call it.'

She frowned at him. 'You are in love with solitude.'

'Is there a better cure for the world than solitude?'

His answers irritated her. 'Where's the cure in that?'

'Where there is no disease, no cure is necessary.'

'I see.' Her eyes narrowed. 'So I am your disease, then?'

He picked up his gun. 'You are my illustration. If I had spent the afternoon alone in my bed, I would not be standing here discussing mysteries when I should be halfway across Wiltshire after a hare.' He leaned down and kissed her. 'Shall we agree on nothing today?'

'Nothing,' she said, determined not to yield.

He called his dogs and went out.

Throughout the winter months there was always a fire and always food on the table, and his presence affected her in ways she barely understood. It would not have occurred to her to ask whether he loved her more than he loved his dogs, and when they lay together she thought of nothing but the fathomless black of his eyes. Sometimes he came to her with great urgency, and at other times lazy with indifference. She watched him when his thoughts were elsewhere, and wondered what sort of creature he was.

Dogman disappeared now and then for a week at a time, hunting further from home. When he was not with her, the urge rose up in her to go. One day in St Mary's she glimpsed Jack across the market square, dropped her basket and raced as fast as she could through the crowd. At the main road, the London mail coach narrowly missed her, braking hard and swerving with near-disastrous results for passengers and horses. The driver shouted that justice would have seen her trampled, but she ran on, and at last turned a corner to see a white mare, lovely enough to break her heart, but not Jack.

So much remained lost.

Their domesticity did not include the influences a woman likes to impose on a man. There were two wooden chairs, a table (solid, foursquare), a few pewter plates, one large iron pot and one small, and woollen blankets and sheepskins for the bed. When the tinker came to the door, she had the cracks in the pots filled, and from the peddler she bought two shirt lengths for him, white linen for new aprons, and a length of soft blue wool for a dress. The ribbons and buttons and velvets did not tempt her, and on the grocer's cart, with the exception of a paper twist of salt, a mackerel fresh yesterday from the sea and a bottle of cider, she spent no money.

The hours they passed together, being neither at night nor in daytime, had a tinge of unreality about them. They owned this time between darkness and light, and it was the perfect time for love, being not much good for anything else. He spoke to her with his low mesmerer's voice, and never asked nor seemed interested in how long she planned to stay, what she would do or where she would go next.

And then in early spring he announced that he would be leaving the following day to visit his wife and child. Pell blinked, but said nothing.

'Where do they live?' she asked eventually, calmly, and when he told her she nodded. 'And why do you go to them now?'

'My son needs teaching to hunt.'

'And she?' Pell could not bring herself to say 'your wife'.

He drew on his pipe. 'I married her when she found she was with child. But I could not live with her then, and I cannot now.'

She had known that his silence contained secrets, and in no way imagined this to be the last. She knew that he did not shrink from experience. And, suddenly, the thought of him leaving filled her not with terror, but a renewed urgency about her own unfinished business.

He left her with meat, salted and stored, a large quantity of flour, the cellar carefully packed with apples and the last of the winter vegetables, and stacks of wood under cover beside the house. He did not say when he would be back. When they parted, he held her gaze, as if about to ask her something, but then smiled, and kissed her lightly. 'Goodbye,' he said. 'I will return when I can.'

His dogs followed him out.

After he left, the little house gradually lost its warmth. Dicken scratched at the door and ran circles round the place when she let him out, ignoring the rabbits in a frantic search for his lost friends. Pell imagined that Dicken was more attached to the familiar than she was, and pitied him, but each morning that arrived without the sound of his return filled her with melancholy. Would it be weeks or months? A single season, a year? She saw herself sitting and waiting, while everything that was hers lay forgotten, and knew that it was time to leave.

Dogman had left some money, and in a mood of opposition she applied to the elderly shoemaker at St Mary's for a new pair of boots. She ordered them stout rather than fashionable, in brown leather, the soles layered with cork for warmth and thick enough to stand up to hard walking. And although grateful for the business, which made a change from patching an endless stream of unsalvageable work shoes, the cobbler disliked her. He knew as little as anyone about the strange woman who came from nowhere and lived with the poacher, but her mere existence filled him with suspicion.

'Things ain't what they was,' he grumbled, pulling a wooden last out of his collection, and measuring her foot against it. 'Half the county moving about, living where they oughtn't. And another half can't be bothered to work. Not when they can live for free on parish funds.'

Pell, who thought she had observed more of workhouses than he had, said nothing.

'Squeezing the parish to pay for every ne'er do well, every simple maid and whatever bastards result.' He glanced at her sidewise, judging the effect of his words. 'It ain't right.'

'It can't be much of a life in the workhouse,' said Pell mildly.

'Bed, fire, two meals a day? Nice enough if you ask me.'

She hadn't, but said nothing.

'And now each parish dumping its poor on the next.' He screwed his face into a disagreeable smile and lowered his voice. 'We sent twelve of them these past months over to Andover. And good luck to 'em.'

Pell sat up straighter. Parishes dumping their poor? She'd never heard of such a thing. If true, it meant that Bean might be found where she hadn't thought to look.

It took nearly a week for the cobbler to complete the job and present her with a pair of tall, shiny, conker-brown boots with sturdy sewn soles, after which she sold her hens at market, paid for the boots in full and rolled her few belongings into a parcel.

One road in, one road out. At the southernmost edge of St Mary's, a stone marker pointed in the direction of Andover. With a shiver, as if someone had stepped on her grave, she set off.

30

Bean had not grown accustomed to life in the workhouse. Instead, he grew thinner and paler and his skinny arms and legs shrank until his body began to resemble that of a child half his age. Hunger and neglect intensified the old-man look about his face. 'Old Man' was what they called him in lieu of a name, and the extremes of abuse he suffered filled his joints and bones so full of aches and pains that the name soon began to describe his condition.

One day, the master and matron walked through the wards, pointing at this child, this youth, that man, and they were pulled out and loaded on to a rough cart and taken on a day's journey to Andover. The talk along the way was of all they had heard about the conditions of their destination, and none of what they had to say encouraged Bean. And yet, up until the moment they arrived he maintained some hope that a new place must offer improvement on his current existence.

What he found made him think of his father's descriptions of hell.

Perseverance seemed the only course of action, and so he did what was necessary to outlast his fate. Crammed together with eighty other hungry, stinking men and boys, he slept on his hard, flea-ridden mattress at night, itched at his angry red flea bites with filthy broken fingernails and ate his thin gruel not because it was palatable, but because if he stopped eating it he would die. His sores bled and became infected, causing his legs to shake with fever when he tried to rise. He did what he was told to do as long as he was able, picking oakum until exhaustion stopped him, or helping to push the heavy handle of the bone grinder round and round until his body failed and he had to be half carried, half dragged back to his pallet.

On days he was too weak to rise, one older boy, whose soul had not yet been squeezed dry of compassion, ate half of his bread ration and brought him what remained. The boy had to be quick to escape Matron's eye, for it was her policy to pocket any unclaimed ration in exchange for the instructional adage that 'no work earns no bread', or 'laziness pays no dividends'.

After an entire winter in Andover, Bean came to two separate realizations. First, that he would die if he remained in this place any longer and, second, that he did not want to die. Having found that there was no hope for him at all in the world inside, he waited for the first mild day, presented himself to Matron, pointed at the door, and watched as she (aghast at his audacity) drew herself up to her full aggrieved height of five foot nothing and saw him out.

'My charitable house is not a prison,' said she, hauling back the great iron bolts of the door, and arranging her face in an expression of utmost forbearance. 'Any one of you is free to leave at any time if that is what you desire.' It was a motto unlikely to inspire her inmates, there being so little prospect for survival in the outside world.

'The boy will be dead in a day,' she told the warden, 'but that's none of our concern. We've done the very best for him, and if he chooses to throw it back at us, we shall have to turn the other cheek.'

The warden did not comment. He never commented, a propensity for silence being all he had in common with the boy who limped off down the road away from him. Bean's head burned with fever, the slightest touch of workhouse clothes against his skin caused him pain, and the bones within his frail body ached. Yet he felt determined to get away no matter what trouble it brought, and he pushed himself on in a frenzy of dread until the place receded from sight.

When he had shuffled and staggered nearly two miles, he left the road and curled himself up like a fox cub in a stand of golden hay, snuggling down in the sweet-smelling grass while the sun beat down and warmed his wretched frame. The smell of warm grass and the sound of birds after months of nothing but captivity, cold and misery, caused in him a delirium of bliss. He fell at once into a deep sleep, in which his mind filled with images of Pell and her white horse. Occasionally he woke, but minutes later would sink back into unconsciousness. For more than a day he lay in his nest of hay, panting, shivering and sweating, more dead than alive. Until finally he entered a place of dreamless rest, and once more waited for his luck to change.

All day long, people passed him on the road, some noticing without interest, others thinking he must be dead, and still others curious at the sight of a child curled up in the grass by the highway. Some offered him water or bread, and a group of gypsy travellers helped him to sit up and eat a nourishing soup, and sip tea to help with his various ills. Upon leaving him, they left word along the road, so that when Esther came to a crossroads, a variety of signs informed her – as another person might have been informed by a telegram or a broadsheet – of the condition and whereabouts of the child.

She laughed a little to herself, and shook her head, and wondered when the intricate game of hide and seek across Salisbury Plain might come to an end.

31

Any attention Pell had earned as a determined runaway paled in comparison to that which she attracted now. Good food had brought colour to her face and a new quality to her figure; she no longer looked so boyish or so young. Her dark-blue dress was new and without worn patches; the apron she wore over it, spotless white. She pulled her hair back and fastened it with a red ribbon as for a pony that kicked, because the thought pleased her. Her boots shone over fine knitted stockings.

Dicken had attained his full size and his head reached her hip. A thick ruff of fur at his neck made him appear bigger than he was, and when she smoothed the seeds and burrs out of his blue-grey coat, he looked ancient, majestic. His puppy capers had slipped away, and he trotted beside her with dignity. Despite a gentle nature, the mere size of him offered protection.

They slept as before in abandoned barns and cowsheds, with money enough to buy bread and cheese and beer. Dicken would eat at her table if she let him, would rather live off bread than catch his own dinner, but despite the reproach in his eyes Pell refused to share her meals with him. The warm days had brought rabbits out by the dozens; they were hungry and somewhat dazed, and made easy prey in the misty dawn.

She stopped occasionally to pass the time with other travellers, or with girls standing outside front gardens, sometimes with a child or two. The encounters left both parties dissatisfied: Pell, tired and homeless; the other women moored in changeless harbours. After a few days on the road, her life with Dogman began to lose focus, blurring into a general picture of a past that included people and places she might never see again. When contemplating the future, the pictures were hazier still, and no single track lay before her. Only two images remained clear in her head: Bean and Jack.

As she approached her latest destination, it began to rain, frozen rain, then hail – balls of ice as big as gooseberries that smashed the ground and exploded, scattering glinting shards in every direction. Pell took cover under the canopy of an ancient chestnut as the bombardment went on and on; it was nearly half an hour before she emerged again into the open, and a wet icy soup underfoot.

Into silence.

No breath of air rustled the branches of the trees, no bird sang. She cast about, discomfited by the absence of noise. Above, on a bare branch, seven magpies sat still as stones, watching. *Welcome to Andover*, their eyes said.

A few minutes later found her at the door of the workhouse. The very air felt cold here; even the landscape fell away at the edges of the building as if anxious to be somewhere else. At a time in which news travelled slowly by coach and infamy built up slowly over decades, the name Andover had become overnight synonymous with abuse and fear. It was known as the worst of the places offering bed and board to the desperately poor, and stories as far away as Nomansland reported that as each load of bones was delivered for the inmates to crush into fertilizer, the poor starving souls fought tooth and claw for whatever traces of stinking meat and rancid marrow remained. And that was not the end of the unpleasantness, so it was said, but the beginning.

She reported first to the warden, a florid ex-soldier. He smiled a smile avid with desire, and she looked away, unable to conceal her disgust.

'Ridley, you say? A mute boy?' His expression was ugly, repaying her dislike in kind. 'I don't think we have one of those.'

She fought an urge to run.

'Of course, if a boy's unable to speak, there's no way of knowing where he might be. Dead and buried most likely.'

Pell flushed. 'May I look, to be certain?'

The man bowed, tucking one hand beneath his stomach, in a mockery of old-fashioned chivalry. 'As you wish, Miss Ridley.'

Despite his offer, he did not move aside for her to pass. Pell hesitated for an instant and it was enough. He was quick, grabbing her arm, digging his strong fingers into her flesh, and drawing her so close that she could smell the onions and brandy wafting up from his gullet.

'The boy isn't here,' he breathed, his face inches from hers, his other hand pressing her against him. 'But I have connections that would make finding him easier.'

Pell held her breath and stood perfectly still, imagining herself frozen, or dead.

'It's not much I'm asking in return.' His voice rumbled low in her ear. 'Just an hour or so of nothing that costs *you*, miss.'

Pell didn't flinch. She met his gaze with her own, perfectly level. 'If you do not remove your hand from my arm,' she said quietly, 'I will cut your throat.'

His eyes widened as he felt the tip of Dogman's knife pressed against the underside of his jaw. He drew away from her slowly, face flushed scarlet.

'You harlot,' he hissed. 'You'll never see your bastard again.'

But she could smell his fear, and knew him to be a coward. Still holding the knife, she walked past him and out of the office door.

It took nearly an hour for her to search the boy's ward. As she walked round the miserable room, she observed heaps of stinking rags, which turned out to be children huddled together for warmth, too exhausted and hopeless to move. Only their eyes followed her. She chose one or two emaciated creatures still with the energy to pluck at her skirt, and asked if they'd seen a child matching Bean's description. One boy with a head like a skull answered that he had indeed seen such a child.

'Never spoke a word, did 'e? They put 'im to work on the crushers, dint they, though 'e warn't likely to live long doin' that sort of work. Delicate thing 'e was, miss.'

'Was?' Pell's heart stopped.

'Gone now, ent 'e, miss?'

'Dead?' Her voice shook.

'Not dead. Left, miss.'

'Gone where? When?'

'Disappeared, not long 'ence,' the boy said. 'Dunno where to, miss.'

Her face fell, and the boy took advantage of the moment to insert his cold, bony fingers with utmost gentleness into her pockets, feeling for bread or coins. He found a scrap saved for Dicken, stuffed it at once into his mouth and looked up at her with burning eyes.

'Being mute, 'e warn't likely to tell us, now, war 'e?'

32

Dogman's wife received him without enthusiasm.

Their son, a half-grown fair-haired lad, hung back in the shadows while his mam made tea, and only emerged when called upon to fetch more wood for the fire. The boy snatched glimpses of his father, torn between excitement and fear.

The pretty woman beside the hearth tended a baby with pursed lips and a pale nimbus of fine hair. 'We called her Winnie,' she cooed, 'after her gran.'

Dogman looked at the baby and nodded.

'Do you want to hold her?'

'I'll leave that to the father.'

His answer didn't suit her. 'What brings you back?'

With a tilt of the head, he indicated the boy. 'Time someone taught him to hunt.'

'Gareth could do that.'

'Could. If he stuck around long enough.'

She puffed out her feathers like a hen. 'Don't start taking issue with him.' She sounded querulous to her own ears, and scolded herself for taking up his bait, and so soon. 'He'll be back any time now. Doesn't stay away so long nowadays.'

Dogman didn't comment.

'And, besides, the boy's at school now. Doesn't need to learn your ways.'

'So you say.' He looked away from her. 'Tom . . .'

She persisted in needling him. 'No one calls him by that name now he's grown.'

He sighed. 'Thomas. You want to come hunting?'

'Yes, Pa.'

'And who's to pay the fine, or visit the lad in prison when he's caught with a doe or a grouse that don't belong to him? I'll not be worrying about transportation neither, do you hear? Won't have my son sent half round the world in chains.' She stopped, wiped a film of sweat from her forehead and leaned her arms and head up against the great wooden mantel in an attitude of defeat. He saw for the first time that she was expecting another child. 'I thought I'd be rid of you by now, and your hold over us.'

Dogman stood up abruptly. His expression hadn't changed, but the dog at his side looked up at him and trembled. 'I'll come at dusk.' As he went out, he heard her muttering her disapproval to the boy, or perhaps to herself.

Every night, Dogman called for Tom and they set off. The boy had to run to keep up with his father's long strides as they walked for miles in the dark. At first it was agony for him, tripping and falling over every ridge and stone, catching every branch in his face or chest. Great sobs of self-pity welled up in him as he stumbled along behind the terrifying figure of this man he barely knew, who marched through the woods in seemingly endless pursuit of nothing at all – for they rarely stopped to draw breath, much less to trap something.

For more than a week the man pretended not to notice Tom's

desperate gait, his ungainly attempts to keep up; for more than a week he gave his son's misery and his clumsiness time to pass. And, much to the boy's own amazement, he began to feel how things were underfoot, began to sense the shape and camber of the ground, and to accommodate it as he ran. Slowly, he found himself knowing how and where a branch would spring back, his eyes detecting shape and movement where before there had been nothing but impenetrable dark. He heard things he'd never heard before, sounds that told him how near he was to water or to stone or how the land dipped up ahead. Now, when he stood perfectly still he could hear birds flying or calling softly; he could hear footfalls that weren't his own. The difference between one rustle and another let him know a bird or a mouse was nearby, or merely the wind. And all this he learned without being taught, merely by following Dogman when he walked, and stopping to listen when he stopped. As he learned more, he began to relax, to walk more quietly and yet more freely, to hold himself less fearfully and embrace the dark.

When he had accomplished this first part of the boy's training, Dogman too began to relax, to know that the job could be done.

On the nights that followed, his teaching commenced in earnest. He taught the boy to lie perfectly still and wait for the moon or a lantern to reflect light on a pair of red eyes. He taught him how to make and set snares for rabbits and foxes, to fasten each trap carefully along well-used paths and adjust the tension to kill cleanly. He taught him to speak to his dogs so they knew what was expected, and would bowl and kill or retrieve the prey, as he liked. He taught him to move silently through dry woods; to catch birds on misty mornings in low nets they couldn't see; to treat a rat bite and draw a goose without leaving a mark on the body; to net dens or flush a badger from its sett.

Each morning he returned the boy to his mother, and disappeared before she could thank him. Which was just as well, as Tom's mother had already paid her penny a day in advance for his lessons, and was angry at the waste, on top of everything else. She didn't know where Dogman slept and didn't care.

The boy learned. Dogman didn't speak a great deal and when he did speak, his son listened. Tom felt proud of his new skills, and though he didn't exactly enjoy the company of his father he began to fear it less. After a month, Dogman felt that his duty had been discharged, at least for the present. At the beginning he had wondered what sort of son he had, but by the end he knew: avid enough, clever enough, willing enough. But enough his mother's son as well, so that he dragged his feet, just enough, unwilling to abandon himself entirely to the job at hand.

One night, Dogman returned the boy at first light and was greeted by the sight of a horse tied up outside the cottage. He recognized it immediately, and sat down nearby with his dogs to wait.

Harris emerged a few minutes later. 'Long time,' he said, grinning.

'That it is.'

'You checking up on your wife?' Harris leaned back against the front of the house with a proprietary air, still grinning. 'Thought you no longer cared.'

'You thought right.'

Harris laughed and shook his head. 'Marion says you've no faith in me to raise your son properly.'

'Helps to show up now and again.'

'Suppose it does. I'm not much good at family life.'

'Damn good at something, though.'

142

'Ain't that the truth.' Harris laughed again. 'Want to drink to my next brat?' He crossed over to his horse and pulled a bottle out of the saddlebag. 'Finest French wine,' he said, tugged out the bung, drank and passed the bottle to Dogman.

'Don't I recognize that horse?'

'This one?' Harris looked startled for an instant. 'You might just. He's one that girl picked out in Salisbury. Good eye she had, all right. Look at him. Turned out handsome, eh?' The deep bay glowed with condition. If it hadn't been for the crazy blaze on the face, Dogman would never have recognized him. 'Often think of that girl. Knew her business, all right.'

'Didn't get paid, though.'

Harris frowned. 'What's that?'

'Didn't get paid.'

Harris kicked at a stone in the path. 'I waited and waited. Girl never showed.' He drank from the bottle again, and looked closely at Dogman. 'What do you know about it, anyway? Hardly seems your business.'

'Girl lost her horse, her brother and five pounds that day. A lot of people got to hear about it.'

Harris squinted annoyance. 'And her spreading it far and wide that I'm some sort of criminal horse-thief child-stealer?'

'Wouldn't you?'

'I'd give her the damned money if I ever saw her again. Not that it's likely.'

Dogman held out his hand. 'I'll give it to her.'

Harris laughed. 'That's a good joke.'

Dogman didn't move.

Harris paused, studying Dogman's face until something in his brain added two and two and came to a conclusion. He burst out laughing. 'Well, well, well. So now you're a one-man benevolent society for the well-favoured needy, are you?' He reached over to slap Dogman's shoulder. 'I see it all now, I see it all.'

'The money?'

Still laughing, Harris disappeared into the house and came back with five pounds. 'If I hear she doesn't get it –' He handed it over. 'That's food straight out of the mouths of babes. Including your own. Don't know how you live with yourself.'

'Nor do I,' said Dogman.

33

So Bean was alive, or had been recently. Pell searched the village and asked at every place if they'd seen a small boy, mute, on his own. But to no avail. A thousand times a day she placed herself inside her brother's head and attempted to imagine where he'd gone. But other than a burning desire to put a distance between herself and this awful place, she felt nothing. Who did he know? At what place would he find shelter? There were no options.

With the exception of Nomansland.

Pell travelled all day and half of the next with Dicken loping at her side, setting out as the first grey light dribbled over the horizon and barely stopping to eat. A hundred times over, she thought of sending word to Louisa, certain that by now she would be pregnant with Birdie's child, and all rancour nothing but a distant memory. The reunion she imagined with her sisters was a joyous one.

When finally she arrived at the edge of the New Forest, she slowed her pace and walked quietly, wrapped in Lou's fine knitted shawl. For the last stretch of the journey she arranged herself with dignity, imagining herself the prodigal son, anticipating welcome.

The Forest foals she'd helped to raise were now sturdy yearlings, and she recognized them with pleasure. Budding hedgerows, woven through with brambles and ivy and still with a supply of red and black berries, harboured a dozen varieties of birds. The sun shone warm against a dark-blue sky; soft grasses swung glowing in the early spring light. She exchanged greetings with one or two people she knew by sight, wondering a little at their faces. Nobody smiled.

It was the wrong time of year to be coming home; a few months later and all the women and children would be out in their gardens. Someone would have run ahead to alert Lou, who might (even now) be rushing out to meet her. Pell rehearsed her return over and over, the forgiveness each would show, the happy couple, even her good-for-nothing pa and poor worn-out mam rejoicing. And, best of all, she saw Bean, having found his way back to the only permanent place he knew, smiling at her from the doorway.

As she walked through the hamlet, however, no one ran to greet her. Women who happened to be out of doors stared as she passed, nodding briefly in greeting, and the children she recognized stopped in their tracks and gaped silently. 'Look at me,' she wanted to say, 'look at my dress, how new it is and how handsome, and my boots, polished and of excellent leather.' She was certain that someone must have run ahead to let her family know she was back; any minute now the little ones would be shouting her name and throwing grubby arms around her. But here she was almost home, and still no sign.

What came to her first was the awful smell of catastrophe, the dampened soil and charcoal odour of collapse.

The house, when she reached it, was ruined.

What remained of the roof had caved in, the side walls lay in crumpled heaps, its front door charred and smashed. What was left of the garden lay heavy under a thick blanket of old ash. Pell brought both hands to her mouth to contain a wail of disbelief. She raced along the road to Finch's, which she found exactly as usual, shutters open, a polite trail of grey smoke curling up from the chimney. Pounding on the front door, Pell stepped back abruptly when one of Birdie's sisters, her eyes wide as saucers, threw it open.

'Mam!' she cried, and Mrs Finch came, meeting Pell with the corners of her mouth drawn down.

'So you're back, are you? Well, I'm sorry for you, I suppose, but you got what you deserved.' Behind her, a figure appeared. The face had a red, unhappy look, with bruised-looking flesh around the eyes, and for an instant Pell didn't recognize him.

'Hello, Pell.' He smiled. 'I knew you'd come home at last.'

'Oh God, Birdie, what happened? Where is everyone?'

'That's a fine dress you're wearing. You're looking well.'

'Birdie, for pity's sake!'

'You been away months.' He spoke to her as if explaining to a child. 'Lou's gone. Your mam and pa both burned to death in the fire. Buried there.' He pointed towards the chapel.

Pell moaned, but he kept on.

'Didn't know where you were, so's to send news. I knew you'd come back, though.' Eyes empty, he smiled again. 'I been waiting.'

'*What happened?*'

He shrugged. 'It started in the thatch, at the back wall, at twilight. A spark, maybe. Your father'd been drinking and your mam was in bed, ill. By the time anyone knew, it was too late.'

She could have smashed his face for the slow way he spoke.

'Lou and the girls were out when it happened.'

'Thank God.' She wept quietly.

'Lou's gone now. Married a man from Lover. Fancy that! Old Mr Bellings.' He grinned mirthlessly as he said the words, and leaned in till his face was right up against hers. '*Old man*. And the little girls taken to Andover.'

She sank to the ground.

'Lou's husband wouldn't have 'em. And no one here to care for 'em. No house, and no money.'

'But couldn't you and Lou –' She broke off and he turned the half-question over in his head, making sense of it.

Slowly her meaning dawned on him. 'You expected *me* to marry her?' He recoiled. 'But it was *you* I loved.'

She looked at him dully. 'There are other girls, Birdie.'

'Who'd marry a fool? That's what they call me. No one'll have me now. Except maybe there's a girl in Lover, not right in the head. Maybe you could tell her family why you had to creep out in the night, because of it being such an awful prospect, marrying me.'

'Birdie, I –'

'But you haven't got another husband, have you, so it's not too late to undo what you've done.'

The ground spun.

'Go on, I'm asking you again, aren't I? I got no place for pride.' He was beside her, had gathered her hands in his. 'Marry me if you're sorry, Pell. Put it right.'

She stared at him, dumbstruck, and he stared back, understanding at last that whatever plans she had made did not include him. His expression froze.

'Just leave here.' Anguish twisted his features. 'You've brought enough sorrow, to me and to everyone else.'

She stepped towards him. 'Birdie . . .'

'Go!' He was shouting now, threatening her. '*And don't come back.*'

She fled.

34

Pell retraced her steps, travelling back to Andover as fast as she could go, praying that one thing, at least, she could set right. She slept only in snatches, starting up each time in torment at the vision of her mam and pa, burning.

On arrival, she went straight to the workhouse. As the warden entered the outer room, she could smell the place in his clothing. Death and depravity, she thought, and it clings to him like a shroud. The smile he smiled at the sight of her made her blood freeze, and she wished never to see a face with that particular expression on it again.

'Well, *well*. Good morning to *you*, miss.'

'I'm here to fetch three children out.'

'*Three* children, now? What a careless family you have. First one child, now three? Are they mutes too? Or isn't that any of my business? No, no, of course not. My business is right here, making a profit from the worthless poor.' He smiled again, this time at the desperate pallor of her face. 'So today it's three children. What a thing. Tell me, Miss Ridley, how has life taken such a turn for the better that you've come to collect *three children?*'

A haze of darkness enveloped her. Her very bones felt worn out with sorrow.

'Heavens above! Another mute! Perhaps that's how the first one came by it. Runs in the family, does it? Like idiocy, they say.' He chuckled. 'Excuse my mirth, miss. I'm just imagining a whole family of idiots. Did you say you were their mother, or their sister? Or perhaps both? You see quite a lot of that in idiot families.'

'Frances, Sally and Ellen Ridley.'

'Of course, Ridley. I remember now. Been here all along, only you didn't ask for girls. Common enough name, of course, didn't occur to me they might be yours. Four children!' He ran his eyes slowly down her body. 'And at your tender age.'

She held her ground, made her mind blank.

'Here we are.' Licking his fingers, he turned the pages of a large ledger. 'If only you'd asked the last time, I'd have led you straight to them. Thought it a bit odd. Never mind, can't be helped. Nothing lost, in any case, as it's only been a few days. Only . . .' He looked up at her with the oily mock-concern of a money lender. 'Oh, dear. We seem to have just two Ridley children listed here.'

'There are three. If you'd check again . . .' Her jaw tightened.

'No need, miss, no need.' He shoved the ledger at her. 'Right here, you can see for yourself, it says here: Sally Ridley, thirteen years old –' he looked up – 'would that be right? Deceased. Just two days back. Of fever.' He looked up at her. 'Of course, everything was done to save her. No expense spared. Finest food and medicine available.'

She gasped.

The warden stood grinning.

'And . . . and the remaining two?'

'Yes, of course. If you'll wait here, the warder will fetch them for you.'

It was nearly an hour before the warder returned, half dragging two creatures by what scraps of collars they had left. Their clothes were filthy and they cringed and cowered.

'Take your idiots and good luck,' snarled the warden, all interest in the game finished. 'They're hardly human, those two.' At a gesture from him, the warder dropped the children to the ground in front of Pell, motioning threateningly with his foot. The warden raised his hand as if to hit them and they recoiled, mewing with fear.

'Idiots,' he laughed, and left the room.

Pell knelt to embrace the girls. 'Come,' she said, noting how tightly the flesh stretched across their bones. 'Come, Frannie, Ellen. I have cakes for you. Would you like cakes?'

They fell upon her, frantic. '*Cakes, cakes!*'

Pell took one hand of each, and pulled them to the door. They had once been big girls of ten and twelve, but now their limbs seemed shrunken. Ellen's dreamy eyes drooped with sorrow and all the spirit had drained from Frannie. Once away, tears streamed down Pell's face, of rage as much as sorrow.

She stopped at the baker's and bought a loaf and some sweet buns, which the children stuffed frantically into their mouths. She would have to take a room for them, but as they approached the inn, the landlady placed herself squarely in the centre of the entrance.

'You're not taking those filthy creatures indoors,' said she, indignant. 'They can sleep in the barn with the other animals.'

Pell protested, to no avail. So she took them to the barn, and with the promise of more to eat, installed them with Dicken in a loose box.

Starvation had reduced them to beasts and food made them

human again. They would eat anything put in front of them as long as there were no bones, retching sometimes with the strain on shrunken stomachs. Dicken stood beside them as they ate and ate until not another crumb would go down, and they gripped on to him, locking their fists in his coat and sinking down into the straw in a stupor of satisfaction. At first Pell tried to slow them down, but they howled until she gave in. When finally they lay asleep in the straw – whimpering, knees drawn up to swollen bellies, fists clutching her dog – Pell watched them sleep and brushed angry tears from her eyes, asking herself the same question over and over: *How could this have happened?*

And then she stopped. She had no leisure to weep over what was past.

She sent a letter to Mrs Louisa Bellings in Lover, hastily scratched, telling her about Sally, and how she'd found Franny and Ellen, and where they would wait for her. The next day she received a reply, saying Lou was on her way. While they waited, the children slept and ate, waking occasionally and crying out, or crying out in their sleep for Sally, cringing as if expecting to be punished for the noise. As soon as she could, Pell washed them clean with the soap used in the stable, an unnerving ordeal that left all three exhausted and dripping. They stayed with Dicken in the box while Pell fetched new woollen cloth for pinafores and linen for aprons. She stitched them bigger than need be; they would not always be so thin.

Lou asked for Pell at the inn and was surprised to be directed to the stable. There, she embraced her three remaining sisters, accepting the cries of the two younger and steeling herself against the place in her arms where Sally should have been, and Bean. Two children found. Two lost.

From within the embrace, Pell whispered in her ear, 'How could you have left them?'

'How could I?' Louisa drew back. 'It was you, Pell. You left, that was the start of it. And then Mam and Pa dead, and no one left to sort out what was left. We had *nothing*, no money to pay the rent, not even the good opinion of the village. When Mr Bellings offered to have me despite all the talk . . .' She dropped her eyes, and when she raised them again the blue of them was like ice. 'What would *you* have done? What would you have had me do?'

Pell said nothing.

'Do you think what I did was for my own pleasure?'

'But Birdie . . .'

It was the first time she had seen Lou angry. '*You left him*, Pell. You left, and you didn't wait to see what happened next. Birdie never wanted to marry me.'

Pell turned away.

'What did you think would happen? There were so many broken promises. Don't you see? It won't ever be put right.'

Pell nodded, her eyes swimming. 'Tell me about the fire.'

35

Lou left the next morning. Her husband expected her back, she said, and it was no use delaying; he would not stand for it. Pell promised to write from wherever they should settle, but refused Lou's suggestion that they return to Nomansland. 'I can't return, Lou. If it were the last place left on earth, I *would not.*'

Lou dared not dissent.

'We'll make our way.'

'But how?'

Pell shrugged. 'By some means.'

Lou shook her head. 'I would have the children if I could, but there's no use thinking of it. Mr Bellings will not.' She thought for a moment. 'His niece works in Winchester, at the Wykeham Arms, on the edge of town. I have met her and she seemed kind. Perhaps she will help you.'

And with that they embraced, and among many tears set off in different directions.

Pell and the children travelled slowly. After ten miles of hilly roads even Dicken stopped chasing rabbits and walked by her side, subdued. As she walked, she thought of her parents, and of Sally and Bean, and though the little girls cried for Lou, she said only that they were going to Winchester. By the time they arrived, all three were footsore and downcast.

The Wykeham Arms was easy enough to find, and although Lou's niece was not in evidence upon their arrival, at the mention of her name the owner offered a tiny room under the eaves with supper not included in the price and Dicken to stay in the stable. It was cheap, and Pell accepted gratefully.

A person accustomed to worse might expect to sleep soundly on a bed within four walls. But the room had no fire and no windows, was musty and cold, and Pell awoke constantly throughout the night. With the girls to comfort and be comforted by, she managed a few hours rest at dawn.

The previous night's dinner of steamed pudding with ham arrived cold for breakfast, served by Lou's niece on a wooden plate, and when Pell said who they were and how they had come, she greeted them warmly, disappearing to the kitchen and reappearing a few minutes later with a glass of warm elderberry wine beaten up with egg for Pell, and hot milk with nutmeg for the children, saying it would do their spirits and their health good. The kindness did more to warm Pell's heart than the drink.

As Pell sipped her wine, she slowly unfolded the story of Nomansland, of the death of her parents and brothers, and Sally, and her search for Bean and Jack.

The girl listened with sympathy. 'What a dreadful story! Will you return home?'

'No,' said Pell. 'There is nothing for us there.'

'What will you do?'

'I shall have to find work.'

'You'll need more good fortune than most to find work here.'

But she gave Pell the names of places at which she might enquire, and wished her luck.

Pell left the children at the inn and went out searching.

At The Bell, she was told they would not take on a girl they didn't know. The King's Head had a livery stable where the man barely graced her request with an answer. The Swan required no new staff, now or ever. At the baker, it was suggested she try the house across the road, where servants were always required due to the bad temper of her ladyship, but there the cook said she'd rather take on a basket of frogs than a good-looking girl with no references, and the housemaid wouldn't consider a girl the cook wouldn't have. The butcher looked so ill-tempered she didn't stop, the post office had a waiting list of local hopefuls (all known and trusted), the grocer had daughters, the shoemaker an apprentice, the carter four sons. And at no time had she dared mention her sisters.

Another day passed. Once more she left Dicken and the girls and walked for miles, enquiring at each substantial house whether anyone required a scullery maid, a cook's helper, a nursery nurse, a groom. Her rejection at each was accompanied by a greater or lesser degree of incredulity at her lack of references, or letters of introduction, or family connections. At last, on the outskirts of town, the owner of a large untidy farmhouse offered her a few days' work sowing and bird scaring. A shilling a day. 'But you'll have to get rid of that dog,' he said, and when Pell turned round in surprise, Dicken stood waiting for the slightest sign of recognition before greeting her with the enthusiasm of a long-lost lover. 'I'll not have any poacher's dog hanging about my chickens,' grumbled the man.

Disappointed as she was, she couldn't blame him.

As she returned slowly to the inn, Pell considered the possibilities. She could go on to Oxford, or apply for employment at the paper mill in Swindon. 'They'll take anyone,' Mr Belling's niece had told her. 'There's fourteen from this town there already.'

What remained? There was always London, with its new factories and its choking smoke, but she was not yet desperate enough for London. She had given up on Harris. Even if she found him, he would certainly have sold Jack. Evidence already confirmed him as a liar and a thief, and without Dogman she had no proof that he owed her money. As the event receded in history, her chances of a satisfactory resolution faded away to nothing.

With these thoughts in her head, she made one final stop, at the forge on the edge of town. She already knew the reception she would receive there – a girl at a blacksmith's shop was an absurdity – but she was drawn to the smell and the sound of it, and the knowledge of how it worked and what she could do.

In the yard, a farm horse stood patiently while a big-shouldered old man held one of the animal's great hooves between his knees.

'Excuse me,' she said softly. 'Excuse me, but I'm looking for work.'

The man paused, holding his heavy hammer on the upswing, and looked at her with a puzzled expression. 'For whom, miss? For your husband or brother? For your father?'

'No,' she said, even more quietly. 'For myself.'

'For yourself?' The smile on his old weathered face broadened. 'Why of course! You may as well start here.' Still holding the heavy foot aloft, he offered it to Pell, chuckling.

'I will,' she said, 'if you'll lend me your apron.'

With a delighted grin, the man put down his hammer, untied his old leather apron and placed it over Pell's head. It dropped heavily on to her shoulders and she hesitated only a moment before wrapping the ties twice round her waist and knotting them in front. Then she picked up the hammer, took from him the four remaining nails, hefted the hoof in one hand and leaned her shoulder against the shire's, in a polite request for him to bear the weight of the leg himself. Being a sweet-natured creature, he complied, and she hammered the remaining nails into the shoe, taptaptap, three taps per nail with perfect accuracy, just as she'd been taught as a girl, straight and smooth, trimming and flattening each neatly where it emerged from the wall of the hoof.

The unfamiliar exercise left her flushed and a little breathless, but it was worth the effort for its effect on the old man. He gaped at her, mouth open, as she lowered the hoof, ran her hand down the great horse's neck and murmured 'thank you', as close to its ear as she could stretch on tiptoe.

When she turned to face the farrier, she summoned up her courage and said in as clear a voice as she could muster, 'I'll do whatever odd jobs you can find for me.' The weight of need compressed her chest so that her voice emerged squashed. 'Anything at all.'

It took a minute for the man to regain his wits. Then he scratched his head and called out, 'Daniel! Who was asking for a boy? John Kirby up at Highfields, was it?' He turned back to Pell. 'Get yourself up to Highfields, half a mile out of town by the post road, and tell John Kirby I sent you. Mind you,' he added with a chuckle, 'I'd give something to see the man's face when you turn up.'

She might have thrown herself at his feet with gratitude, but settled for an expression of thanks so earnest, the old man flushed with pleasure. As she and Dicken headed off in the direction he indicated, he stood watching, hands on hips. 'Of all the things,' he muttered, still grinning and shaking his head. 'Daniel! Did you ever see such a girl? Of all the things.'

At Highfields, Pell headed straight for the smart-looking stables and asked for Mr John Kirby. A groom directed her to the tiny office at the end of the aisle, where records and pedigrees were kept in huge leather-bound books, and a serious man in a smart green jacket, black boots and white breeches sat sorting invoices and receipts. When he looked up and saw Pell, the expression on his face changed at once.

'Well,' he said, standing to greet her, 'you may be just about the last person I expected to see today.'

'Is it . . . are *you* John Kirby?' She stammered, recalling at once their meeting on the road to Salisbury fair. 'I . . . it was the smith in town who sent me, if you please. He said you were looking for a boy.' She blushed. 'For someone to help in the stables.'

'Well, I was, and I am,' replied Kirby, 'but I wasn't imagining that the someone who turned up would be you.'

'Nor was I expecting *you*,' she said, venturing a smile, for she was more than pleased to see him again. 'And did you find a good home for the chestnut mare . . . for Desdemona? I have wondered about her many times since.'

He smiled. 'Aye, to as soft-handed and meek a young lady as you can imagine, and I hear that they have never had an instant's trouble with each other.' He shook his head. 'You never can tell with horses.'

'I'm happy for them both,' Pell said, but her voice quavered with trepidation.

'And you?' John Kirby said at last, sitting back and frowning a little. 'You'd better tell me by what fateful route you've arrived here from Salisbury fair.'

'Please,' she said, and it seemed as if her entire body inclined into the word, 'please consider me for the job. It is one I can do.'

His face attempted to accommodate both a grin and a frown, arriving at neither satisfactorily. Instead, he shook his head, and indicated that she should sit down.

'Now, then,' he said.

He listened carefully as she recounted the bare bones of her story, from Bean and Jack's disappearance to her arrival here. She left out her time with Dogman, saying only that she had lived in a barn near the town. At the end he shook his head. 'You're not frightened of the world, are you?'

She answered softly. 'I have not had the luxury.'

'Well,' he said after a moment, 'I was looking for a boy, from one of the big houses by preference, with experience of the job and good references.' He tapped his fingers on the desk, musing. 'But a decent boy isn't easy to come by these days, and your experience is certainly . . .' He paused. 'Unusual.'

Neither said anything for a moment, and then John Kirby pointed at Dicken, who lay silent and polite at Pell's feet. 'He's your dog?'

She nodded.

'There's nothing more, is there?'

She could tell that her story caused him to consider what he was taking on. 'Yes.' Her voice was almost a whisper. 'There is.'

He waited.

'I have two children, sisters. I am all they have left in the world. They would have to accompany me.'

John Kirby watched her carefully, watched the colour rise on her neck. 'I see,' he said.

Tears pressed at her eyes.

'I must think about this.'

She nodded. A long silence fell. She knew he was thinking of a way to say no, and prepared herself to hear it, squeezing her eyes shut against his words.

'You would have to work hard.'

She looked up.

'And keep the dog out of trouble.'

In the moments that followed, Pell felt tempted to beg and plead and swear commitment, but she said nothing. Despite what it cost her, she merely nodded, and waited.

'Well,' said John Kirby at last, a willing loser in the game of nerves, 'I require a reliable boy who'll work all day, and half the night if it's called for, who's good at his job and can handle the horses with problems as well as the others, who won't over-sleep or drink or cause trouble, who doesn't require much in the way of pay, at first in any case.'

Pell listened intently.

He continued. 'I have a child of my own and sympathy for your troubles. The children can stay, but —'

'They can work!' Pell half rose and spoke quickly. 'They're hard workers, and accustomed to horses.'

John Kirby nodded. 'So I will take you on, all of you, for two months, as a trial.' The expression on her face made him smile. 'Now come and have a look at the place,' he said, and stood, leading her up to the room above the hayloft, which was snug and comfortable, a world away from the stinking hole in Osborne's dairy. When they encountered another of the grooms, she greeted him soberly, and John Kirby watched her. 'You are not attracted to trouble, are you?'

Pell stared back at him, defiant.

'I did not say you were, but it's as well to ask.'

Twenty-four horses were stabled below, and he introduced each to her with a precis of relevant details: who in the household rode or drove which, what sort of feed each required, what exercise. All were housed in large, airy boxes, twelve on each side of the aisle. Iron hayracks held green hay that wasn't dusty, and the straw underfoot looked deep and clean. The feed room smelled of bran and maize and oats, the tack room of leather and beeswax. In each of these places, Pell radiated such an intensity of contentment that John Kirby could feel it simply by standing beside her.

Privately, he felt pleased with his latest employee, with her quiet manner and graceful figure. Despite the unexpectedness of her.

36

Pell collected Frannie and Ellen from the inn and moved them all to Highfields, to the room in the hayloft above the barn. On the way, she stopped at a house with a great crowd of children playing games out in front and offered their mother the brand-new pinafores she'd made for the girls in exchange for outgrown breeches and shirts. It was an odd request, and if the newness of the wool had been less alluring, the woman might have refused on that basis. But in the end she relented, and Pell dressed the girls in worn breeches and shirts, so they would not draw attention to themselves around a stable. She cut their hair short, which neither child much resented, and together they looked like skinny boys with big eyes and open expressions.

The welcome John Kirby offered was bemused. Instead of the pretty little girls he'd imagined, Pell arrived with two ragtag creatures – three if you counted the dog – that might have been boys or girls or anything in between. He frowned, and wondered what sort of witchcraft Pell practised to have convinced him to take them all on, in addition to the hound. But he had already discovered that he had no stomach for refusing her and, in any case, something in her expression defeated his intent.

There are men who will on no account trust their horses to a female groom, but John Kirby was not one of them. He consulted Pell when it came to the handling of a horse that baulked, or bit, and although she never offered an opinion before it was required, she would tell him quickly and without hesitation what she thought. Often, the horses he found troublesome presented no challenge to her; she could refit a saddle to stop this one napping, talk a hunter into going clean over hedges, stop a chewer from chewing or a bolter from bolting – merely by changing what it ate, or how it was tacked, or shod, or ridden, or spoken to.

On arrival, she put Frannie at once to grooming and left her to work her way down one side of the row. Ellen was deathly frightened of horses, and nothing Pell could say would change her mind. Horses had delivered the bones to Andover each morning, the stinking wagon unloaded and then reloaded with the daily dead.

So Pell set her to cleaning tack, showing her how first to use a soft cloth across the surface of the soap with a bit of water, rubbing it into the old leather and wiping down the result. Ellen rubbed hard, removing sweat and wax and dirt until the harnesses shone like new. Next she buffed saddles, one after another, swooping across them with long smooth strokes of stiff boar and soft badger brushes until the leather shone with a rich mahogany glow and her thin arms ached. Harness brasses needed careful rubbing with vinegar to clean, and iron bits were rubbed and polished like silver. And when John Kirby's son toddled into the barn in search of his father, Ellen lured him out from under the perilous hind feet of the horses and sat him next to her in the tack room, talking and telling him stories until his mother came to fetch him home.

Relieved of grooming, Pell went to work. She applied oil to forty-eight pairs of hooves, closed off the mouse holes in the feed bins, scrubbed every manger clean, and at the end of each day piled them high with new hay, swept the wide oak floorboards clean and refilled every bucket with fresh water. With the three sisters employed sun-up to sundown, it wasn't long before every corner gleamed bright as day.

While Ellen could not be near a horse, Frannie could not be kept away. Within a week of their arrival, she began to rise at dawn, standing on a box to heave the heavy saddles on to horses whose withers she could not reach. She galloped the ones that required exercise, nearly invisible in the flow of a mane, while Kirby watched with trepidation. Only the sweet perfection of balance kept Frannie safe, for she was not strong enough to exert force against an animal weighing nearly a tonne. Kirby could barely bring himself to look, so certain was he of disaster, but Pell stood beside him in a trance of admiration, reliving her own days of being fearless and free.

The three sisters worked for the privilege of having work and of being together, with only Pell's pay as a reward. And still John Kirby worried, and wondered if he'd done the right thing. But even he had to admit that the work was done, and done better than before, and that it didn't cost him more than it had before, and perhaps it was his tidy mind that added up the figures and couldn't come to any sum that didn't favour himself.

The two little girls with chopped-up hair and angel faces charmed the entire household: one with a calf's soft eyes, the other an agile, grinning imp. Even the most dangerous horses settled for Frannie, who was the master's favourite, and who could blame his attachment to the pretty boy-girl with flashing brown eyes and the same voice as her sister for calming a nervous beast?

Ellen watched everyone and knew everything, and if a tool or a farthing or a bootjack went astray you had only to ask her where it might be and how it got there. With everyone else occupied with horses, she stood a little apart and saw the patterns in life; she was happiest with everything in its proper place, and every person too.

One morning John Kirby arrived early to find Frannie mounted high on Midas, a tall bay thoroughbred of excellent breeding with an unpleasant habit of seeking to remove – by whatever means possible – any rider who settled on his back. In hopes of saving the life of the person foolhardy enough to mount him, he was always ridden with an arsenal of restraints: double bridle, curb and martingale. Despite this, his temper expressed itself in a spinning shimmy with such vertical intent that he was constantly in danger of toppling over backwards upon his rider. If, for some reason, this failed to unseat the annoyance, he would accelerate to a gallop, drop his head between his forelegs and somersault forwards. So he was suicidal as well as angry, and Pell agreed with John Kirby that he must be sold at once.

She agreed, that is, until it came to her attention that Frannie had been riding him each morning with nothing but a headstall to guide him, galloping and whispering in his ear the entire time, then sitting back and settling him into a walk as smooth as cream.

'He doesn't like the curb,' she told Pell. 'It hurts his mouth.'

And that was that.

When night fell, the sisters slept together on one straw mattress. Pell promised she would never again leave them, but a kind of panic flared whenever she was out of their sight. Ellen, especially, woke howling for Sally and Mam at night, unable to settle until Pell pulled her close on one side and Dicken stretched out along the other. Frannie dreamed of Midas and it quietened the echo of crackling fire and cracking bones, but Ellen smelled smoke and the stench of burnt flesh every time she closed her eyes, and refused to be comforted.

It would be untrue to suggest that John Kirby never imagined his own wife gone and himself embracing Pell, taking on the two little girls for his own. But it went against his better sense (and he had no shortage of better sense) to fall under the thrall of a young woman with so complicated and unconventional a past, and so he did not.

37

The stables felt more·serene than anyone could remember. Horses trotted out smartly and rarely turned up lame. Reins slipped smoothly through gloved fingers, leaving no mark. And when the sisters mounted the stairs to their little room each night, the barn below glowed with something no one could quite name.

As time wore on, however, John Kirby began to notice something in the quality of Pell's work that disturbed him. She was entirely present, he noted, when she looked at a horse, testing a shoulder for stiffness or a saddle for comfort. But for the rest of the time she seemed distracted, absent. He could detect a void in the very outline of her.

When she had worked for him two months, he called her into his office.

'Sit down,' he said, and noted that she trembled. 'You needn't worry. I have no complaint of you.' He handed her an envelope containing her two months' pay.

'It would be a great satisfaction to me if you would stay at Highfields.' He spoke slowly, watching her. 'Your gifts are indisputable, and you have shown the most perfect attention to every detail of your duties.'

He paused.

'But I have noticed lately –'

Her face froze and she stopped him. 'I cannot give up hope of finding my brother. But unless you have information on where he might be –' She met his eyes, and her expression softened. 'Please do not distress yourself on my behalf. You have helped us too much already.'

He nodded, reluctant to leave the matter, but she stood abruptly and returned to her work, with her pay and the security of more months ahead. She tried not to think of Bean.

John Kirby went home that night to his cottage on the estate and sat down to dinner with his wife and son as he always did. He loved them tonight as he always loved them, and it was a sense of his own luck in life, and hardly any other feelings, that caused him to have an idea.

A sale had been announced on a farm ten miles away. John Kirby knew the estate and the quality of the horses and, besides, Highfields was two horses down and the master required a new hunter.

He travelled out early in the day, on his own. Of the animals for sale, a sturdy eight-year-old Irish cob caught his eye.

'Never puts a foot wrong,' the farmer told Kirby. 'He'll carry fourteen stone, but I'd trust him as a lady's mount, or to carry a child. Does what he's asked, and always jumps clean.'

Kirby liked the look of him, found him calm and good-natured, and worth more than the thirty guineas asked. Though the hunter satisfied him and justified the trip, he strolled down the aisle of the old barn, searching for something else. When his eye settled on a fourteen-year-old grey mare, strong and sound with a fine head, he knew instantly that he'd found what he sought. In his head he proposed a good price for the two, and without explaining that the money for the mare was his own, he left with both horses in hand.

Pell ran out, as usual, to meet him and examine his latest acquisitions, and Kirby held his breath.

'He'll do,' she crooned, ducking down to feel the hunter's knees. Then she turned to John Kirby and frowned, running her hand along the mare's neck, from her poll down to the long, sloping withers. 'But we don't need another mare. Nice as she is.'

For an instant his confidence wavered, but the next moment Pell was beaming at him. 'And yet . . . she's a beauty. I can see why you lost your heart.'

'She's for you,' he said.

Pell stared at him.

'Aye,' he laughed. 'You'll need a good horse if you're determined to roam the countryside searching for your brother.'

'For me?' She was like a child, and could not hide her joy. But in an instant her expression turned grave. 'I cannot accept such a gift.'

'You must,' he said, shoving his hands in his pockets. 'For I'll not have her back.'

She met his eyes for a long moment, and then suddenly, as if the wind had shifted, relinquished her dignity and threw her arms about him in a transport of happiness. He embraced her lightly, like a child.

'What is her name?' whispered Pell, too affected, almost, to speak.

'It was given her by the farmer,' John Kirby answered. 'Owing to the way she takes a fence. She's called Birdie.'

Pell almost cried out. But immediately an expression of resolve settled on her features. It was bad luck to change the name of a horse, but she was finished with luck. 'Never mind,' she said. 'I shall call her Grey.'

38

The following week, John Kirby had an order to send three horses and a groom to Milbrook, a grand estate in the next valley, where the master had been invited to join the hunt. It wasn't an unusual request and Kirby sent Pell in his stead, for she had often heard of Lord Hayward's magnificent stables and was anxious to see them for herself. She rode Grey, led the hunters, and took Frannie with her for company on a dun gelding named Marly. Dicken trotted along behind.

At Milbrook, in the splendid tack room with its mahogany and brass fittings, the grooms sat together awaiting the call for new horses from the field. Pell could barely sit still, and had spent the morning wandering up and down the long aisles of the barn, admiring as impressive a collection of horses as she'd ever hoped to see.

When the call came at last, the grooms set out on to the field, hoping the changeover to fresh mounts might occur with a minimum loss of ground. If they planned properly, there would be a few moments of flurry, accompanied by shouted instructions for girths and stirrup leathers to be mended, strained backs to be rubbed with liniment and loose shoes seen to by the farrier. The excitement multiplied when a group of riders came in together, which was when a hoof inevitably came down on a groom's foot, a flask spilled and tempers flared. Today, a big chestnut kicked out as a pony swung too close, catching a groom in the chest and causing a commotion. Everything had to stop for the injured man, and the hunt had already galloped a quarter mile across the next field by the time the riders set off again. Waiting with the injured man to be taken away, Pell felt thoroughly rattled.

It took more than an hour to strip an exhausted animal of tack, walk him dry, groom, feed, water and bed him down. After that, there might be a lull of another hour or two before the order came to set off home again. Waiting to return to Highfields, Pell exchanged talk of rides and riders with the other grooms. Across the room, along one wall, a series of small framed watercolours caught her attention. There were more than fifty of them, hung in rows, each a perfect small jewel of a portrait in the manner of Stubbs.

'It's the eldest daughter of Lord Hayward paints them,' a groom told her. 'Fine likenesses too.'

'Aren't they lovely,' Pell murmured, pointing to one or another of the horses they'd seen out in the field. Frannie examined each critically, thinking, That hock's too long as she's drawn it, or, The look in that eye isn't quite right.

Each portrait revealed some individual touch. Willow had been painted in mid-air over a big brush hedge. A tasselled, hooded falcon sat on a branch above Fez, a red Arab with a high crest and tail. Pell lingered over each picture, until, as she neared the end, she started back with a little cry.

'What have you seen?' asked Frannie.

'Look,' she said, peering closer, trembling, and Frannie's mouth opened wide in wonder. It was Jack, and she would have recognized him even if the artist had not dabbed the black mark the size of a penny on his left flank. 'Please tell me,' she begged the assembled company, her voice quivering with excitement, 'does anyone know him? Does he belong here?'

'He's one of mine,' said the groom just behind Pell. 'Out today with the field.'

Pell stood utterly still.

'His mistress is just sixteen,' continued the boy, 'and as graceful a rider as you'll find in three counties. But it's an odd story. Lord Hayward bought the animal from a councilman – says he found the horse, just like that, wandering the countryside. Sent word out and waited for someone to claim him, with no luck. The luck was his, I'd say. A horse like that, with no owner? There's something else to that story. In any case, *she* believes it was providence, and is devoted to the beast; mad for hunting, and the horse just the same, and if there's a gate or a hedge to be jumped . . .' The groom's words flowed over her, a river of noise, babbling away as her own thoughts raced elsewhere.

In her mind's eye, Pell could see the culmination of her search, the reunion she so dearly desired, and she rejoiced at the thought of how soon they might be together. And then, without her sanctioning them, her thoughts went on to picture Jack's life of comfort and good food and affection, the young girl's happiness. She further imagined the moment she would make her claim, inform the girl, point out the mark on her horse's flank, recount her story and plead for what still belonged to her, while the girl wept in dismay and Lord Hayward stared stony faced and ordered her off the premises or proposed to take the claim to the local magistrate for a proper judicial hearing.

In a state of agitation, Pell paced up and down, filled with fear and hope in equal measure. What would she do, or say? It wouldn't be long before the riders began to drift in. Heart pounding, she rehearsed conversations in her head, practised different outcomes, wrung her hands and, when half an hour had passed, watched as a flushed and smiling girl with smooth chestnut hair led Jack in. Pell cast about, and seeing that Jack's groom was momentarily busy with another horse, stepped up beside her. 'Shall I take him for you?' she asked softly.

'Thank you,' said the girl, and sighed. 'What a perfect day. We galloped to Milton Bend and back round again. You should have seen the size of the gates, and a wall that frightened me so completely I shut my eyes! And then the hounds made the kill just three miles from here.' She ran an affectionate hand down Jack's neck and handed the reins to Pell, who accepted in a kind of trance. Jack greeted her as if they had been apart only hours, with a shake of the head and an affectionate nudge. To Pell he looked bigger, sleeker. Good feed and grooming, she thought.

'He's very beautiful.'

The girl looked at Pell and beamed. 'Yes, isn't he?'

Pell led Jack to the box with his new name on the door, unbuckled the throatlatch and girth, and handed bridle and saddle to his groom, who had arrived at last looking somewhat lathered himself.

'I'm sorry,' he said. 'It's always five horses at once and only so much a man can do.'

She nodded and stepped back, watching Jack, who stood with eyes half closed as his groom sponged him down. Pell recognized that expression of near-bliss, could feel the groom's hands on her horse's knees and shoulders as if they were her own. The thought that he pined for her was laughable.

175

She stood and watched him until her presence was required for one of her own horses. And then she walked away and left him to his new life.

After that everything changed. Her restlessness increased, infecting everything she did or said. She lay awake at night and moved through each day hollow-eyed with exhaustion. Everyone at Highfields seemed real to her except herself. Even her words came to her at the wrong pitch, as if they'd travelled too slowly and dragged themselves through mud along the way. All of the strength she possessed went to pushing against ordinary events, surviving on everyone else's exhalations of air. She lived now only for the possibility that somewhere Bean might still be alive.

Her work suffered. Only she noticed at first, but eventually John Kirby saw that something must be done. He asked to speak to her and she tendered her resignation at once, forestalling his carefully rehearsed questions. There were tears in her eyes as she spoke. 'I feel as if I shall never be able to repay you.'

'Then stay.'

Speaking almost in a whisper, she replied, 'I cannot.'

He sighed. 'Perhaps, when you've found him, you will return.'

'Perhaps.'

For a long time neither spoke. 'Where will you go? How will you live?'

She looked up at him, her eyes clear. 'I will manage,' she said, and knew it to be true, because she always did.

And so John Kirby accepted her request, as he had accepted all her requests. It made him sad to think of what she would do, and his life without her.

In the night, Frannie crawled up close to Pell's ear and

whispered in a voice tight with emotion, 'I don't want to leave here. Midas needs me.'

'We cannot stay.'

'But why?'

'We must find Bean.'

Frannie thought for a moment. 'Couldn't you find him?' She spoke slowly. 'Couldn't you find him and . . . bring him back?'

Pell shook her head. They could not return here.

She could not.

John Kirby wouldn't hear of keeping Grey. But he would employ Frannie, and gladly, until such a time as Pell sent for her or she, herself, returned.

If Pell had not already become accustomed to sorrow, she might have found herself unable to leave Highfields and Frannie. Incessantly, it seemed, life plagued her with responsibilities, made her fall in love, ripped away any consolation she might find. Sisters and parents, brothers and horses. Dicken and John Kirby. Birdie and Dogman. Even Pa's awful house with the tilting floor. All staked their claims on her; each conspired to weigh down her soul. As soon as she accepted one set of circumstances, another leaped up to mock her. Nothing stayed the same. Every day brought unwanted connections, losses and complications that broke her heart.

She reached down and felt for Dicken, on hand as ever to push the ground away as it rose up to meet her. All she never wanted to feel clawed at her heart.

She and Ellen set off.

39

What a procession they made: the grey mare, the shaggy dog, the girl child with cropped hair, and Pell, who had lived two months in breeches and boots, and had only now, with some reluctance, gone back to dressing as a girl. Together they comprised a fraction of a circus, not quite a family, part of a menagerie. The pieces missing from each description left great gaping holes that Pell could not, in her mind, work out how to fill.

They walked and they rode. Dicken raced ahead until Pell called him back and chose another path. Ellen walked slowly at the rear, humming. She would still not sit on a horse. Slowly, they made their way to a place where two roads crossed. A sign pointed in one direction to London, in three others to Salisbury, Winchester, Southampton. Pell stopped and turned to Ellen.

'We'll wait here,' she said.

'For what?' asked the child.

'For something to happen.'

Ellen wondered, then, whether the sister whom she loved and whose judgement she trusted above all others had taken leave of her senses. But she was tired of walking and glad for an excuse to rest, and so they rested. By day they waited and watched the world go by, cooking on a smoky fire while Grey cropped the rich spring grass. By night Pell saw the moon grow fat and felt the tug of it on her own changing body. The sisters lay close together for warmth and looked up at the stars and slept and dreamed of a time they would no longer wander the earth, searching for lost things.

With each person who passed by, they shared greetings and news, and announced that they were looking for a boy, and described that boy, and then waved goodbye and waited for someone else to pass or for silence to fall once more. They talked to farmers on the way to market pulling carts or in wagons, young men on the way to meet young women, ladies in fine coaches and girls in simple traps, couples on foot, old men on ancient horses, shepherds driving sheep. It was a busy highway, and everyone had something to say, though no one had seen a boy this tall with sleek dark hair and no voice.

Day after day, Pell clung to a stubborn confidence. When Ellen looked at her enquiringly, wondering where they would go next, Pell stroked her hair and straightened her clothes, and asked her to help skin a rabbit or boil the potatoes left by the man who passed by this morning, or cut the bread bought from the baker on his way to all the villages along the road.

They waited three days, and then three more, and three more. And then halfway through the next three they heard a low growl. And suddenly there was not one grey dog but two, and a joyous reunion, two grey-coated wraiths melding into one. Pell searched up and down the four roads and around the bend to find the source of Dicken's doppelganger, and then all at once he was there, the gypsy boy with long legs and bones as sharp as Dog's.

'Eammon!' Pell ran forward to him, unable to conceal her joy. She had waited, and kept her nerve, and they had come. 'Where is Esther?'

He grinned at her crookedly. 'Not far.'

She could see the wagon now, a half-mile down the road. Eammon would give nothing away, and so she mounted Grey and urged her on to meet them. It was not until she had nearly reached the caravan that she recognized the driver sitting at the front with Esme, holding Moses' reins in his two thin hands. He climbed down, and she flung herself off Grey and caught him up in her arms, burying her face in the familiar smell of his hair. Esme shadowed them, standing as close as she could to Bean without embracing Pell herself, shyly and a little resentfully reclaiming his hand at the first opportunity. She had not forgiven Pell for losing him once.

'Odd creatures,' Esther muttered.

Pell's eyes met hers over Bean's sleek head. 'So,' she said, 'you found him.'

Esther nodded. And then, all in a rush, Pell told her of Dogman and John Kirby and Andover, and the trip to Nomansland, and everything that had not gone as expected. When she spoke of the fire and the death of her parents, her eyes filled with tears and she turned away, but Esther's expression did not alter. Both women were silent for a long time.

'And did you accomplish what you set out to do?' Pell asked at last, looking at the other woman closely.

'Yes,' replied Esther, with her odd smile. 'I met the man I sought all these years, and talked with him, and then I tapped my pipe out on his house.'

Pell stared, uncertain what reply this strange information required.

Just then, they were interrupted by the reunion of Ellen and Bean and Dicken and Dog, and Pell smiled to think that the circus was, at this moment at least, a step closer to completion.

They stayed together for a week, camped beside a river. Pell told Esther over and over about the terrible fire in Nomansland and the terrible scene with Birdie, until the real events became just another story. Esther listened without comment, and only sometimes looked away with an inscrutable twist to her mouth. On the second day, Pell called Bean to her, which meant she also had Esme, and pulled him close and told him about Mam and Pa and Sally all dead, and Lou married, and Frannie left behind with the horses, and he listened with the most serious of serious expressions, while Esme – nearly as small and big-eyed as he – reached out and gripped on to his hand.

And then Pell asked if he would come with her and Ellen, or stay here with Esther and Esme, and his big eyes widened, and he grasped Esme's hand tight. And Pell saw that there would be no parting them, nor would she try. For a moment Bean gazed at her with a particular expression, not of happiness, exactly, but content. And when Pell saw that he had found his place in the world, a great heaviness rose out of her chest and dispersed in the pale blue sky.

Ellen, for years an invisible child, now came to the fore. She and Pell were the last remaining unclaimed members of the clan. They had each other, but nothing and no one else.

What next? Pell asked herself, unable to give voice to her wishes and fears. She had solved one quandary, only to be faced with another. John Kirby had said she could return, but even as she considered it, she knew that she would not.

The next day, she would give a small book of bird drawings to Evelina, say goodbye to Bean and hand over what money she had left to his mother, inadvertently repaying a lapsed family debt. Esther, whose home was a wagon with a canvas roof laid on to ribs, a shire horse, a hundred square miles of back garden and a clutch of children, would once more set off across Salisbury Plain.

That night they all stayed together and ate from the same pot, animals and children both. And when they slept, they slept as a single family comprised of like, rejected and unmatched souls.

Pell and Esther were the last awake, sitting up late into the night saying not much of anything, while all through the countryside, stories spooled out in soft exhalations from every house or hut under the night sky.

40

Pell planned their journey carefully. They walked quickly, stopping only to eat and drink, and occasionally to rest. They spent a night near Amesbury, and continued on early the next morning. When at last they arrived, she left Grey and Ellen together at the house with Dicken, and walked out alone to meet him.

It took only a few seconds for his dogs to know she had returned, and to run and greet her with wild sweeping tails.

He emerged from the kennels, expecting something but not this, and stopped when he saw her, tilted his head, looked again and, utterly composed, or so she imagined, waited for her to speak.

'I've come back.'

He nodded slowly. 'So you have.'

'I didn't know whether I'd find you.'

He frowned. 'Where else should I be?'

She said nothing.

'I told you I'd return.'

'You did.' Her voice trembled.

'And you couldn't find it in your heart to believe me?'

'No.'

'You have no experience with faith.' It was not a question.

She looked around, from the house to the kennels to the cowshed where she had once lived. 'No.'

He turned away, to the job he'd been doing.

'I've come to ask if you'll have us back.'

'Us?' He dumped a carcass and a bucket of entrails among the dogs, and the frantic clamour subsided to snarls and grunts.

'Us.' She took a deep breath. 'I've brought a horse. And Dicken. And one of the girls.'

'What girls?' He bent over a bucket of clean water, not looking at her. His bloody hands left long pink swirls in the water.

'My sister.'

'What have you done with her?'

Ellen had already emerged, not taking her eyes off him until she reached Pell and grabbed on to her skirts. She peered out, fearful of change, of being left behind. But Dicken lunged at him with such an excess of delight, such a full wriggling rage of happiness, that he had no choice but to say the dog's name, and wrestle him down, and return the greeting.

The child watched, encouraged. But then he turned to her frowning.

'Who are you?' His face was stern.

She took a deep breath. 'My name is Ellen . . .' But immediately faltered. 'Mam and Pa are dead and there's just us now.' She looked to Pell, searching desperately for a reason he might accept them. 'We're all very clever with horses,' she said, remembering, proud of the fact. And then, with a pang of conscience, 'Except for me.'

He struggled to maintain his frown. 'I have no horses. What use will you be to me?'

Ellen pondered the question for a long moment, frightened and resentful all at once.

'What use will you be to us?' she asked at last, a little uncertainly, and Pell felt a surge of pride. The girl's eyes were coal black and wide with anxiety, but there was the spark of something in her that would not be dominated.

'That remains to be seen,' Dogman said. He turned back to Pell. 'Well? What use will I be to you?'

'We could find out. If you'll have us.'

He considered this. 'Have you? As what?'

'As . . . what you like.'

He didn't answer.

'I am so tired,' she said softly.

He stood, motionless, surveying the little group. The scrawny, defiant child with her sister's big dark eyes. The dog. The pretty mare. The girl who was no longer a girl.

'All right,' he said at last, without changing expression.

'Yes?'

'Yes.'

'You'll have us?'

'Yes.'

'You're certain?'

'What answer did you expect?'

'I don't know.' She searched his eyes. 'Why will you?'

'Why will I have you?' He paused. 'Because you'll have me. It's the same for both of us, don't you see?'

She thought for a minute and shook her head. 'No,' she said in a whisper.

He turned to Ellen. 'Are you hungry?'

The child looked at Pell. She was always hungry, of course she was. But it wouldn't do to own up, and to this man, a stranger. Pell closed her eyes to hold off the feeling that might any minute sweep her away, and Ellen, unable at the last to contain herself, or to be truly frightened of him, squeaked, 'Yes, please.'

'All right, then,' he said. 'Let's go in.'